SEVEN CORPSES ALL IN A ROW

MOLLY SUTTON MYSTERIES
BOOK XII

NELL GODDIN

Copyright © 2024 by Nell Goddin

All rights reserved.

No part of this book may be reproduced in any form or by any electronic or mechanical means, including information storage and retrieval systems, without written permission from the author, except for the use of brief quotations in a book review.

ISBN: 978-1-949841-24-4

EPIGRAPH

"We forget how dangerous nature can be. We want to forget, I think. We don't want to be reminded that nature is more deadly than man.

Man can be cruel, but nature is indifferent. It is the unrivaled psychopath."

—James Renner

I

I

October 2008

FLORIAN NAGRAND, longtime coroner of Castillac, mumbled an excuse to his assistant Matthias de Clare and stepped out of the office. He was terribly restless and had not been able to hit on anything to calm himself—not lunch, not walking around, not cigarettes. Though he persisted in employing those same strategies nonetheless, having no idea what else to do.

He sat down on the stone step and took a pack of Gitanes out of his shirt pocket. He shook a cigarette out and lit it, drawing deeply, then shot out a plume of smoke.

He told himself that he felt better, and tried to believe it.

The mild roar of a scooter caught his attention, and he glanced down the street to see Molly Sutton headed his way, her wild red hair mostly hidden under a helmet as she nimbly zipped down the narrow street and between parked cars to stop in front of him.

"Bonjour, Madame Sutton."

"Bonjour, Florian. You're looking like the very picture of despair this morning."

"You would too if you had just gone to see about the second corpse in a week."

"I thought you hated having nothing to do."

"Equally I hate having anything to do."

He took a long pull on the cigarette and fixed his eyes on an empty yogurt cup in the middle of the street. "See that?" he said, gesturing at the cup. "This is not France. Yes, *tais-toi*, I'm generalizing—but in the main, French people don't throw garbage on the street like this. We like things tidy. But this is how it is now. Those bankers in America—see what they've done? They've not only caused widespread global panic, but now your average Castillacois is so dispirited he's throwing empty yogurt cups on the street."

Molly looked at the cup and considered this. "It's true, the financial news has not been good. My bookings are way down. People are nervous."

Florian made a noise that sounded like a cross between a bark and a choke. Molly figured if he had lost the power of language, perhaps it was time to move along and come back another time.

Well, maybe just one question....

"So—you know I'm going to ask, so here goes—anything troubling you at all about this sudden spate of deaths? I know we had a long stretch with no one dying except for poor Benoit LaRue, but... just wondering, it's probably nothing...two deaths in the same week? If my information is correct, the victims were not already sick or otherwise compromised, yet they were suddenly struck down out of nowhere?"

Florian stubbed out his cigarette, carefully put the butt in his pocket, and shook a fresh cig out of the packet. He didn't light it but stroked it with his fingers while deciding what to say.

"First: two deaths are not a 'spate,' and second: I don't know when Selma is coming back. If ever."

"Oh, Florian."

"I suppose I was nothing more to her than a summer fling. Just a playmate for a short while, then tossed away like an empty yogurt cup."

Molly came closer and put her hand on Florian's shoulder. He was sagging as he sat there, his whole large body in one big droop, and she felt his sadness as though it were a physical weight pressing them both down.

Florian heaved an enormous sigh. "As for the two deaths, as you likely already know, one had a heart attack and the other, liver failure. They were not spring chickens. Make of that whatever you wish, Molly, though as usual, I will take the position that there is nothing whatsoever to be made of either death beyond the natural expiration that humans—regrettably, or perhaps blessedly—cannot avoid."

"What about the fact that they are both women?"

"Two does not make a pattern, Madame Sutton. As I don't have to tell you."

They stayed there for some quiet moments. Florian's presence was so heavy it was as though he were slowly sinking into the stone step.

"Is Selma in touch? Has she emailed?"

Florian's broad shoulders rose into a mighty shrug. "What good is email?" he said.

Indeed, thought Molly. Impulsively she kissed the top of his head before heading back to her scooter.

2

Saturday was Changeover Day at La Baraque, the day the current guests leave and the new ones arrive, with all the organizing and cleaning and getting ready that that entailed. Molly's gîte business had slowly improved, year after year, but the fall of 2008 was proving to be more challenging. The decision to open such a business had been, as was typical of Molly, somewhat impulsive; she had never considered that being dependent on tourism meant that when economic times went sour, so would her business.

It seemed obvious now, but there was nothing to be done but wait it out.

Constance, Molly's once-a-week housekeeper,

showed up on time, noisy as ever, full of chatter about the latest person in the village to get divorced and why can't men control themselves and did Molly think when men did not control themselves who was at fault really, was it only the men but what about the women they did not control themselves with?

As usual, no amount of coffee was enough for Molly to withstand the barrage of Constance energy. She had learned to listen, pause for a moment, then pick up some cleaning supplies and get moving.

"You raise large questions for this time of the morning," she said when at last Constance paused to draw a breath. "While I consider them, I'll take the *pigeonnier*," said Molly, grabbing the vacuum and a bucket. "Isn't the weather magnificent?"

"I suppose," said Constance, disappointed that they weren't settling in on the sofa with coffee for a nice long gab. "So who's coming today? You said bookings weren't doing so hot."

"They're not," said Molly. "The entire financial world—globally—is on fire right now. So—and I don't blame them—people are huddled at home and skipping vacations until this blows over."

"IF it blows over."

"Okay, if. I take an optimistic view, always. Because you might as well not go through the day as though the world is ending when it hasn't yet."

"If you say so, Molls. I've been thinking, maybe you should get a cow."

"A *cow?*"

"We could share the milking. It'll eat the grass in the meadow and we get free milk and cheese."

"Ah, I see. Who's going to be making that cheese, though?"

"We'll figure it out!"

Molly laughed and headed to the meadow path on the way to the pigeonnier. The last guests had left early and Molly had judged them to be neat and tidy, so she hoped the cleanup would go quickly. She was meeting a new guest—the only one coming this week—in Castillac for a tour of the market.

Life goes on, she thought. Whether it's global financial meltdown, war, natural disaster—in the moment, it feels like we're doomed, it's all over. But then, somehow, maybe miraculously, at least so far—it isn't.

In the back of her mind, there was a little scritch-scratch of worry, that the current problems could mean the end of La Baraque's being able to sustain her and Ben during the slow investigation times. But she brushed that off, because truly, what good did worrying do?

Molly arrived at the Place, the center of Castillac, having driven her scooter with perhaps ten percent more care than usual, and took off the helmet Ben had implored her to begin wearing. She hated the helmet. It was hot. It was heavy. The effect on her hair was deeply unfortunate.

But Ben, with uncharacteristic vehemence, had insisted, pressing the new reality into her mind—she was no longer Molly Sutton, wife, gîte owner, and occasional detective. Since early summer, she was Molly Sutton, all of those things, plus—amazingly and quite unexpectedly—expectant mother. And that meant making some adjustments. She and Ben were keeping the news a secret, at least so far, so as to enjoy the fact of it by themselves without any village commentary. And perhaps, though neither said it out loud, they were reluctant to tempt fate.

She tucked the helmet under one arm and headed to the statue in the center of the Place where she had arranged to meet the new gîte guest, a Ms. Rolanda Jones from San Francisco. On the way, she saw her friend Manette and stopped for a quick chat.

"What a spread!" said Molly, gesturing to a neat

pile of the red kiri squash, the cauliflower with bright green stems, and several boxes of mushrooms that she couldn't identify. "How've you been? It's been weeks since I've seen you."

"Bonjour, Molly. I figured you'd be off doing your detective thing, what with all these deaths lately."

"Eh, it's only two!" said Molly, waving her hand in the air. "Not every death is a murder, despite the entire village thinking that's my deepest conviction. We do all meet our end someday, after all." Her face turned a light shade of pink thinking about what Florian would say to her sort of quoting him, just after she'd been making inquiries about those very deaths.

"Indeed! Now have a look at my squashes, I'm particularly proud of them. All local. Perhaps you might make a soup for this week's guests?"

They chatted for a few more minutes until the line behind Molly had several people in it, and she moved on to the statue to look for Rolanda Jones.

"*Hola*," said Molly, seeing a woman who matched Rolanda's description of herself: tall with long dark hair in a braid down her back.

"Hola? Aren't we in France?"

"Don't know where the Spanish came from," said Molly with a laugh. "Brains are strange, aren't they? Anyway—bonjour Rolanda! So good to meet you and welcome to Castillac. Before we head back to La Baraque, let's make the rounds of the market, if you're up for it?"

"Absolutely," said Rolanda, grinning. She had a scattering of freckles across her nose and a cheerful, open expression of being up for just about anything.

"I've been to the vegetable stand already," said Molly, gesturing to the two big squashes in her basket. "How about some cheese?"

Rolanda danced into the street, raising her hands in the air and hooting, her dark braid swinging. An aged French man nearby stared as though he had never seen anyone dance before.

Molly led her to the stall of Lela Vidal.

"Her stuff may not look that impressive," Molly said to Rolanda in English. "She doesn't have a wide variety of cheeses, and they're not wrapped in fancy paper or anything. It's not like going to a specialty store—it's just one kind of cheese, you can get it with chives or without. Absolutely exquisite, either way. Do you like goat cheese?"

Rolanda nodded. Molly nodded to Lela, who took a small wooden spatula, like the kind for eating cups of ice cream in a school cafeteria, and dug into a container of dense, bright white soft cheese.

"*Goutez*," Lela said to Rolanda, and Rolanda did.

"Oh my LORD," she said, mouth still full. "Can we just buy everything she has? This is…this is *amazing*. The perfect tartness. So creamy. Just…*ohh*. Am I in heaven? Because I think I just died."

Molly beamed. To her mind, almost nothing was more endearing than a true enthusiasm for French food.

Lela was smiling too, as well she might. "She is pleased?" she asked Molly in French, rhetorically.

Molly beamed as Rolanda closed her eyes, savoring every last molecule of the goat cheese.

"I have all kinds of news from the farm," said Lela. She was not usually chatty but Rolanda's enthusiasm had had an effect. "Have you heard that I bought the pasture next to me—that old brute Monsieur Roulon at last relented and let me have it. I had to pay a ridiculous price. But—it is mine now," she said. "So at long last I have been able to expand, and the goats are extremely happy in their new space, so fresh and green. It has not been grazed in many years."

"Congratulations!" said Molly. "I don't know that I've met M. Roulon."

"You have missed nothing."

Molly snickered.

"He keeps to himself," said Lela, rather darkly.

"Back in the States, that's what the neighbors always say when someone has been arrested for something especially gruesome."

"You must come some afternoon and watch *Tempête* work the herd. I know you love dogs, and you just can't imagine the joy of Tempête as she harasses the poor goats. They are not like sheep and they do not love being bossed around!"

"I would love to," said Molly.

Molly felt rude chattering away in French when Rolanda couldn't understand, so she paid for several containers of cheese and said her goodbyes to Lela.

"Now what?" Molly asked. "No visit to the market is complete without dropping by Patisserie Bujold. Do you like pastry?"

"Is the Pope Catholic?"

Molly didn't expect to love every guest, but this one was already feeling like an old friend.

MOLLY GOT Rolanda settled in the pigeonnier and went to find Ben, who was fixing a broken window in the annex.

"All well?" he said, relieved that she was back in one piece. If he had his way, she wouldn't be riding on the scooter at all, not in her condition.

"Rolanda is my kind of people," said Molly. She stood and watched Ben fit the pane of glass into the frame and start softening the putty. "She nearly lost her mind in Patisserie Bujold. I think she scared Edmond a little." Molly laughed. "Anyway, I ended up getting an enormous box of pastries. We will be forced to gobble them up before they get stale."

Ben stepped back and judged his work, then turned to Molly and put his hand on her belly. "Have I told you how happy I am lately?"

"This very morning," she said, grinning.

"I don't think I can hold the news in an instant longer."

Molly considered. "If people were observant, they'd be able to tell!" She looked down at her thickened belly. "Maybe they just think I've finally overdone it with the croissants. But yes, I know, I've been cautious about sharing the news."

"It's not like you. Not that there's anything wrong with it."

"It's just...well, you know. I never dreamed this would happen," she said, patting her hands on either side of his. "Never in ten million jillion years. So if anything happened?" She rapped her knuckles on the wooden window frame. "I wouldn't want to have to go through that grief with all of Castillac watching."

"Nothing is going to happen," said Ben. "I know this to be true. Absolutely one hundred percent *know* it."

Molly smiled at him, then reached a hand to his cheek. "I guess, now that I think about it, not telling goes against my principles. Just this morning I was lecturing Constance about not dwelling on bad things that are possible but haven't happened yet, and what have I been doing but exactly that."

"Not dwelling, exactly, I wouldn't go that far."

Molly shrugged. "But not assuming the best outcome, either. I'm putting a stop to that right this minute."

"So that's a green light? We can spread the news?"

"Green light," said Molly. "Frances is going to kill me for keeping it secret for over four months. She'll say: you don't treat best friends that way—and I see her point. Let me tell you, when I've been holding baby Luka it was almost impossible not to tell her. I'm not sure I have ever in my life demonstrated so much restraint."

"How about dinner at Chez Papa tomorrow night and tell everyone then?"

"Perfect plan," said Molly. She had a queasy feeling in her stomach, but queasiness had been a daily thing for months and she had come to accept it.

Ben went back to puttying the window and Molly stood and contentedly watched for some time before drifting back to the kitchen and that box of pastries.

3

It was a brisk Sunday morning, the autumn breeze sweeping out the last vestiges of Indian summer, and Molly and Ben decided to go for a walk in the forest. Bobo sprang ahead and zoomed behind, covering fifty times the distance of her humans as she chased rabbits and smells and other delicious mysteries. Ben took Molly's hand and they walked without speaking, feeling nothing but pure happiness.

Molly felt her phone vibrate in her pocket and ignored it.

Ben heard it and gave her a quick side-eye, but kept walking.

Molly drew in a big breath. "The forest is so peaceful," she said finally. "You could walk on this path and believe that living things exist together in harmony, with no idea of the fierce battle for survival going on, from the wild boar all the way to the beetles."

"Profound thought for an ordinary Sunday morning," said Ben. "And grisly, I might add."

Molly laughed. "I just mean—nature—it's not all rainbows and cute bunnies, is it? We want to think of it that way. And it *is*, I mean of course there *are* cute bunnies and rainbows and all manner of beautiful and wondrous things. But also…in a way…nature is fearsome. Always, eventually, for every living thing—deadly. I don't mean that in a morbid way. Only that from death comes life and then death again—there's no avoiding it. Maybe we're wrong to fear it so much."

Ben spun her by the hand so that they stood facing each other, and leaned in for a kiss that went on for some time.

"I'm really looking forward to bringing the little one into the forest," he said. "I want to get one of those backpacks he can ride around in."

Molly squeezed his hand and they kept walking. But of course she had not forgotten the vibrating phone. Eventually her fortitude wore thin and she let go of Ben and reached for it.

"Sorry," she said, looking at the screen. "Oh my."

"What?"

"It's from Matthias. Someone died."

She shoved the phone back in her pocket and kept walking.

"Well? You going to tell me who?"

"Lucien Pugh, I don't know him, do you?"

"Not really. I know who he is. Probably in his early sixties? Quiet sort, as far as I know."

Molly tapped her lip with one finger.

"Not the kind of guy you'd expect to have enemies," added Ben, giving her a look.

"I'm not thinking anything!" Molly laughed. They could just see bits of the blue sky if they looked up through the trees, and both of them, without saying so, felt as though they wanted to be in the warmth of sunshine again. So Molly whistled for Bobo and they turned back, while Ben told Molly everything he knew about Lucien Pugh, which turned out not to be very much, or very titillating.

※

"WELL, WHAT?" said Frances, when Molly and Ben came into Chez Papa just after dark. It was a beautiful October evening and it seemed as though the entire village was out to enjoy it. The barstools were all taken and there was only one empty table.

Baby Luka was only six weeks old. Frances was standing at her usual place at the end of the bar, the baby in a carrier against her chest, and you could just see two little feet sticking out the bottom and the top of Luka's head in a wee knitted cap.

Molly went straight to Frances. "Bonsoir, sweet Luka," she said, giving one of the tiny feet a squeeze. "What are you shouting about, Franny?"

"Well, I'm sleep-deprived, you know. And that makes me just a hair less patient than I usually am."

Molly snickered.

"So listen," said Frances, "I am absolutely sick and tired—I mean *sick and tired*—of you keeping whatever secret you're keeping. Do you think I can't tell? I've known you since first grade, Molly Sutton. And when you're holding something back, it's completely obvious. Even Luka can tell."

Molly smiled. It was a good feeling to be known so well, even if it meant secrets were hard to keep. She waited for Ben to come over after saying hello to Lapin and his wife, Anne-Marie, who were sitting at the other end of the bar. She waved to Edmond, who was making a rare Sunday night appearance, since bakery hours had him up in the middle of the night, with no nights off.

Ben slipped his arm around Molly and looked at her. "Go for it," he said softly into her ear.

"Frances," said Molly, and then her throat closed and tears welled up and she shook her head.

"*What?* Do you have cancer? What *is* it?"

Ben was dying to jump in but restrained himself. Molly swallowed hard, wiped her eyes, and said, "It's unbelievable, I know. I still can't believe it myself. I'm pregnant."

Frances just looked at her blankly.

"No joke," Molly added.

"Not a joking matter." Frances frowned. She had heard what Molly said but the words were stuck somewhere, not understood.

"Definitely not." Molly made a strangled noise that was a mixture of laugh, bray, and sob. Ben rubbed her back, his face lit up in a way Frances had never seen before.

It started to sink in. "Are you *serious?* How in the world did this happen?" said Frances, her eyes widening.

"The usual way," said Ben with a small smile.

"But I thought—"

"So did I," said Molly. "So did I. Several doctors—not just one—told me there was no hope. They didn't say the chance was small. They said it was zero."

"And yet..."

"And yet."

Frances reached her arms around Molly and squeezed as tight as she could without squashing Luka. "This is...this is beyond the beyond, the best news *ever!* Absolutely amazing!" She buried her face in Molly's neck and then tilted her mouth up and let out a howl of joy. Luka startled and uttered a tiny cry, then settled back, nestling against her mother, not seeming to mind the noisy hubbub of the bistro.

Nico was busy but kept looking over as he made drink after drink, wondering what had his wife so worked up. Finally he was able to come to the end of the bar, kissing Frances and then Luka on the side of their heads while setting a kir in front of Molly. "So? Who died?"

Everyone stared at him.

"Lucien Pugh? But you've probably already heard that," said Ben.

"Right, I just thought, with all the excitement over here, there must be more bad news..."

"Actually, this time? It's birth we're talking about, not death," said Molly.

"This is better," said Ben.

"*Much*," agreed Frances.

"I am with child," said Molly. "Against all odds."

His eyes got wide.

"Okay, don't you people be sharing all the

gossip over here and not letting us in on it," said Lapin, forcing his big self into the group and pulling Anne-Marie with him.

And then, never one to be left out, Edmond Nugent wedged himself in as well, along with a few people that Molly did not know, just because the energy was so charged up and happy and anyone would want to be a part of it.

For at least an hour, it was as though Molly were holding court, with all manner of Castillacois —friends and strangers—coming by to pay their respects and give congratulations for the little one on the way.

"This is so unexpected," she murmured to Ben as another old man she didn't know tottered away after kissing her grandly on both cheeks and squeezing her hands as he spoke of his happiness at her news.

"What?"

"It's...well...in the States, at least as far as I knew, having a baby is strictly a friends-and-family sort of thing. This is seeming more like, I don't know, like I just scored a winning goal for Team Castillac and everyone in the village is cheering for me. I feel so..." She got choked up and didn't finish.

A middle-aged woman with a braided bun approached, looking shy.

"Bonsoir, Albertine," said Ben gently.

"I just wanted...to give you...my fondest congratulations on the event," said Albertine, looking all the while at the floor.

Ben was about to answer when someone shouted, "*Va-t'en!*" in an ugly tone. Ben turned to see Milo Clavel theatrically throwing a scarf around his neck and glaring at a woman seated at a table. Milo narrowed his eyes at her. She looked down at the floor, not going away as he had ordered, but not firmly standing her ground either.

They were a middle-aged couple, not married —past the usual age of tempestuous and public carryings-on, thought Ben. He wanted to go to Delphine and put a supportive hand on her shoulder, but did not want to inflame Milo further by taking sides.

Chez Papa got quiet. Everyone was watching to see what Delphine would do.

DELPHINE DID NOT MOVE. Her body was completely still and her head stayed at the same angle, looking down. As though she were a mouse in the forest, hoping to blend in with her surroundings so that the fox would not see her and move on.

"She used to be one of the beauties of the village," Lapin said to Anne-Marie in a low voice.

"Not anymore," said Frances, not shouting but nevertheless still too loud.

Milo stormed out, slamming the door, and several of Delphine's friends went over to console her.

"Charming man," said Molly.

"*Chérie*," said Edmond, taking his second turn with Molly, the new Queen of Castillac. His eyes were wet. "I wish you every happiness. Do I understand this is unexpected?"

"Completely," said Molly. "We were getting ready to adopt, actually."

"I've heard that often happens," said a woman with soft brown curls and a big nose.

"Will you proceed with the adoption as well, and make it a regular zoo out at La Baraque?"

"Maybe," said Molly. "We'll just have to feel our way along." She was looking at the door, wondering if Milo was hanging around outside or had really taken off. "Tell me about Delphine. I can't understand how I keep meeting so many new people this many years into living here, but I do. I've never seen her before."

"Ah, for good reason," said Edmond. "She only just moved back to Castillac after being away for many years. She grew up here, her family has always been here...but she had a bad breakup years ago and moved to New York City."

"That's a long way. The breakup must have been horrible."

"Sometimes it takes a big move to get on with your life," he said pointedly, knowing Molly had done exactly the same thing. "Anyway, Delphine didn't come back for years, not even for a short visit. Married someone in New York, had some kids...she's only been back now for a month or so. I believe her husband died not long ago. And unfortunately, she has gotten together with that execrable excuse for a human, Milo Clavel."

"I've seen him around. Never talked to him."

"Skip him," said Edmond, and his expression was serious.

❧ 4 ❧

First thing Monday morning—and never mind the rather foggy head from celebrating at Chez Papa the night before, which had dragged on into the early morning—Lapin pulled his truck into the white gravel driveway of the solid, middle-class house of Lucien Pugh, deceased only the day before.

Some Castillacois, maybe most of them, were concerned about the recent number of deaths in the village. Three in just a couple of weeks. For Lapin, however, death was an opportunity. It was from estate sales that he acquired most of his inventory after all, having realized early on that usually, the relatives of the recently passed on did not drive nearly as hard a bargain as the sharks who inhabited auctions and even flea markets.

He had been called by Lucien Pugh's nephew the day before, practically minutes after Lucien died, and hired to assess the belongings in the house and dispose of them for the family. A job Lapin accepted with pleasure, and wasted no time in starting.

"Bonjour, Lapin. I'm going to leave you to it," said the nephew, coming out of the house the minute Lapin's truck pulled up. "I'm sure you don't need me lurking about and looking over your shoulder while you do your job. I trust you, of course. Just tell me—how does this process work? Do we meet to talk about your findings? I don't expect that my uncle has anything of particular value."

"Oh, you never know, you just never know. Often a family has no idea that some piece of furniture or odd trinket that has been passed down through the generations has become in demand. That's one of the interesting things about antiques —it's not a static, unchanging list of what's precious and what is not. Value changes because tastes change, you understand?"

The nephew's eyes were beginning to glaze over; he was interested in computers, not old furniture.

Lapin saw the flash of boredom and hurried along. "As for this process, we can handle that however you like. I'll write up a list of items with approximate valuations, and then you can decide which things you want to keep. I'll give you a list of options for what to do with the remainder, which will depend on what's here. We can do this in person or over the phone. Or email, if you'd prefer."

Lapin had found that people's responses to a death in the family were as varied as the infinitude of ice cream flavors. This nephew, he thought, was quite standard so far, a plain vanilla. Though his calling on the actual day of his relative's death was a little out of the ordinary. Vanilla with hazelnuts.

The nephew drove off and Lapin went inside. It was not a large house and the inside was tidy. He stood for a moment in the living room, letting the surroundings sink in. There was a history magazine on the table beside the armchair, and Lapin imagined Lucien sitting there reading it only a few days earlier. Lapin might see village deaths as an opportunity for business, but that did not mean he was callous about the event or what it meant to the friends and family left behind.

For Lucien Pugh, there were not many of either. But one does not need a lot of friends to have a good life, Lapin thought. Really, just one good friend will do, and Lucien certainly had at least that.

He walked from room to room, taking note of the larger pieces of furniture, checking to see if there was anything valuable tucked somewhere, which did sometimes happen even in modest houses. He stopped at a bureau in the bedroom and looked at an array of photographs in brass frames. Who were these people, Lapin wondered, not recognizing any of them. An old photograph, perhaps from the 1920s, showed a woman in the sort of bathing costume popular then that must have caused some drownings, it was so bulky and heavy-looking. Another photograph of a man with impressive mutton-chops, looking sternly into the camera.

Lapin noticed that everything was quite clean, the place was dusted and swept. So if there *was* anything valuable, he guessed it would have been well taken care of.

He heard someone fiddling with the door and strode back to the living room.

"Ah, André! Nice to see you."

"Bonjour, you old grave robber!" André said, clapping Lapin on the back after they kissed cheeks. "Where's the nephew? We were supposed to meet here at ten."

"Long gone, I'm afraid," said Lapin. "You're the *notaire* on the job?"

"Indeed I am. I advised Lucien years ago on the applicable inheritance laws—you know well what a convoluted web that can be, if you have much of an extended family! Though Lucien didn't have much in the way of family—I believe the nephew is pretty much it—but he was a man who liked to make sure everything was done properly. I don't think there are any other beneficiaries waiting in the wings, though you never know what people might be up to, do you?" André said with a laugh.

Lapin chuckled. "I suppose you must see all manner of behavior, in your line of work. People falling out over inheritances, for one thing."

André just shook his head. "I'm sure it's the same for you. Money and greed—oh, the trouble they cause." He walked into the small kitchen and opened the refrigerator. "I see the situation's well in hand—already cleared out the refrigerator and turned it off. Now that's a young man who's on the job!"

Lapin shrugged. "So he inherits everything?"

André swept his hand across the room. "Everything does not amount to much," he said, shrugging. "But maybe you'll find some gem hidden away somewhere."

"Maybe," said Lapin. And if I do, I'm not telling a soul, he thought. He scratched his ribs, thinking about it. Well, he would have to tell Tom, of course, there would be no living with himself if he didn't. "All right!" he said heartily. "Let's see what Lucien's got."

※

DELPHINE'S HEAD WAS THROBBING. It was nine in the morning when she staggered out of bed and made her way to the kitchen, took a tray of ice cubes out of the freezer, and then pressed a cube onto her forehead, then her temples, and then the back of her neck.

"It's really not cool, at your age," said her nineteen-year-old daughter Daisy, coming into the kitchen and standing there with arms crossed. Daisy had on sleek all-black workout clothes and looked like the New Yorker she was.

"What's not cool," said Delphine, wanting more than anything to curl up on the floor but resisting as long as Daisy was there.

"That nasty hangover. I'm going for a run. Catch you later."

Delphine put a hand on her belly, trying to quell the nausea. She had had too much to drink last night, there was no arguing that point. Not that she needed her daughter wagging a finger in her face about it.

Daisy was on the small front porch and closing the door, when suddenly she jerked the door open and stepped back inside. "And one more thing, *Maman*. That dude you've gotten with, Milo? Just *no*. Daddy must be rolling in his grave. And yeah yeah—before you tell me Daddy is dead and has no say in the matter, okay fine—but I'm going to spell out the obvious: that dude is *bad* news. Get rid of him. Holy hell—please—get a freaking clue."

The door slammed and Daisy took off down the street at a fast clip.

Delphine sat down on the cheap sofa and put her head in her hands.

Her daughter was right.

But did she have to be so rude about it?

Maybe coming back to Castillac was a mistake. But once her husband died, New York no longer felt like home. If it ever had. At least in Castillac, she had old friends to rely on, thought Delphine, who had realized, in middle age, that friendship was more valuable than romance.

Were there any sour pickles in the fridge? They can get rid of a hangover, if you could only keep them down.

5

Molly sprang out of bed the next morning ready for action, though with only one guest who was all settled in, there was not a single thing on her to-do list. She lay back down next to Ben, trying to simply relax and listen to the chatter of birds, but her mind was tearing this way and that and would not be calm.

"I'll make breakfast," said Ben, slapping his feet on the floor. Bobo dashed in and leapt on the bed, licking Molly's face.

"I got some goat cheese on Saturday, I'd say let's have some of that on toast but I somehow managed to lose it on the way home. Last week I lost my keys and spent an hour looking for them—

they were in my hand. I think this baby is slowly sucking the last of my brain cells right out of me."

Ben laughed. "You have a few to spare," he said.

"Generous of you."

"You say that as though there is something wrong with generosity." He laughed. "Scrambled or fried?"

"Fried. There might be some leftover potatoes to go with, if you look behind the milk."

On the bedside table, Molly's phone vibrated. She picked it up and took a long look at the screen. "It's Matthias," she said, almost too softly for Ben to hear. "There's been another."

෴

THE FRIED EGGS were left behind as Molly got dressed, hopped on the scooter (not forgetting the helmet), and went straight to the coroner's office.

"Bonjour Matthias," she said, waving to him once she was inside. "And bonjour to you too, Florian. I see your mood has not improved."

"Why would it?" said Florian, who was leaning heavily on his elbows, on the verge of face-planting on his desk, which was piled with papers. "We're suddenly flooded, horrifically flooded. We do nothing but work from dawn into the night, day after day. And after the work is done, nothing but a cold, empty house to go home to."

Molly exchanged looks with Matthias. "No word from Selma?"

Florian only moaned and let his forehead drop to the desk with a thump.

"Okay, well, sorry to hear that. Now then. Let's just stipulate the usual objections to my being here, shall we?" said Molly. "I have no standing, it's none of my business, etc., etc., etc. All agreed to, check-check-check. If you give me five short minutes, I would merely—as a citizen of this lovely village, you understand—request a bit of clarity about the victims. Nothing deep, nothing thorough, just the bare bones. If you would."

Florian scowled. "I'm going out for a cigarette," he said to Matthias. "If the phone rings, don't answer it."

"That's one benefit of working in the coroner's office," Florian said as he and Molly went outside. "It's not like we're Emergency Services and so much depends on not losing a minute hustling to where the trouble is. For us, the trouble is already over. And to the poor victims, when we get there doesn't matter so very much. At least most of the time."

"I'm glad you feel you're in the right place," said Molly.

"Just call me Dr. Death," he said, settling on the one step and taking out a pack of Gitanes. "Want one?"

"Quit years ago."

"Of course you did. You do realize that former smokers are among life's worst people?"

"Weren't you a former smoker for a long time?"

"I am one of life's worst people, for a number of reasons. This is not news."

"Oh, Florian. I would try to say something to make you feel better about Selma, but I know that would just be irritating."

"Indeed it would."

"Okay. Subject change. Piles of dead people. We're up to four now, in two weeks? Is my math correct?"

"It is." He struck a match, watched it burn.

"I am not acquainted with her biography. But no, I believe she was here visiting someone. Not local."

Molly nodded to herself. "Three lifelong residents of the village, one from out of town?"

"Correct."

"Two women the first week, and two men the second."

Florian took a drag and held it in. He looked at Molly and shrugged.

"Causes of death?"

"You're really very annoying, you do know that about yourself?"

"I do." Molly grinned and patted him on the shoulder.

"I shouldn't be telling you any of this. You have no credentials, no—"

"I thought we stipulated all of that at the beginning."

Florian tapped the ash off his cigarette and took a long drag. "Oh, I missed you so," he murmured to it, and then took another brief drag. "I wouldn't give you the smallest scrap if it weren't..."

She patted his shoulder again. Molly had learned about Florian that he responded better to touch than words.

"...if it weren't for the Benoit LaRue case. You...you sort of saved my bacon that time," he muttered.

Molly shrugged. "Eh, you hadn't really done anything so wrong. I'm happy if my part in it was a help to you. I mean that."

"Ah, don't be getting sentimental on me, Sutton, after the couple of weeks I've had, that would be the last straw."

"Okay. Then—just quickly—run down the causes of death. I know you've already told me about the women. Are any the same? Just curious."

Florian shook his head. "You're not going to be

able to make rhyme or reason out of it this time, I'm afraid. Let's see. One had a heart attack. Another, liver failure. Third, kidneys went. And the last, I'm sad to say, had a fatal case of diarrhea."

"Oh dear."

"He was a hundred and four. The dehydration got him."

"Well, that's quite an array." Molly sat, eyes unfocused, tapping her chin with one finger. "Not a duplicate cause among the four." She sighed. "What's your impression, Florian? You're saying definitely, one hundred percent unrelated? Being relatively close in time is the only thing the four deaths have in common?"

"That is my conclusion, yes." Florian looked up at the ceiling and waited.

"Well, I suppose statistically…it's certainly understandable that we'd get a flurry of deaths. After going so long without any. It's not like we can expect people to die once a month like clockwork."

"Indeed. I'm glad to hear you aren't having dreams of serial killers."

"I'm not having dreams of anything. Four deaths in that short amount of time *is* unusual, you have to grant me that much. I just wanted to have a little chat about what's been happening to see if… see if…well, you know."

"You make it sound as though dead people

need to clear their deaths through you before going on to the next world."

"Maybe I should design a special stamp."

"For the caskets?"

Molly threw her arm around Florian and they laughed until tears came.

"Tell you what, I will email Selma this afternoon," she promised. "Just to see what she's up to."

"Don't tell me anything about it," said Florian firmly.

"Oh, stop being such a man."

"Molly, chérie—I have no choice in the matter."

Molly stuck her head back inside to say goodbye to Matthias and give him a wink, then back to La Baraque. She drove the scooter so slowly no one would have recognized her, as her mind was entirely taken up with the four corpses and their four causes of death.

6

"I'm just going to come right out and say it, Molly." Lawrence adjusted the napkin in his lap and glanced out of the window of Cafe de la Place, where they were having lunch.

"Yes...?"

"I feel..."

Molly cocked her head. She waited. Lawrence said nothing.

"You feel what? Honestly, Lawrence, since when are you tongue-tied?"

"What I want to say...it's not attractive, I know. So I resist saying it out loud. But here it is: now that you've met Matthias, and you're all best buddies and everything, and he's your direct line of intel from the coroner's office—I feel so...unnecessary. For years I've been the first to give you notice of any new deaths. And now? I'm superfluous. Tossed aside like yesterday's newspaper."

Molly couldn't help it, she laughed.

"See what talking about feelings gets you around here," he muttered, with a hint of a smile.

"I do miss hearing from you every time someone in the village moves on to the next world."

"Is there a next world? I wonder."

"Don't we all. Anyway—I don't need to tell you you're being silly because you already know it. You're my best friend in the whole village, along with Frances. Not just in the village—anywhere. And that friendship, as you know perfectly well, has nothing to do with texts or the coroner's office or any sort of information, no matter how juicy."

It was a busy lunch crowd and Pascal, looking as movie-star handsome as ever, finally came to take their order.

"Molly, I heard the news and just want to tell you how thrilled I am for you," he said, leaning down to kiss her cheeks.

"Thanks," said Molly, who at that point had had just about all the congratulations she could take. "We're really happy. I'll have the *boeuf Bourginonne*."

"Can't go wrong with that," said Pascal, not writing it down.

Lawrence ordered the same and Pascal went through the swinging doors to the kitchen to place the order with his mother, the *chef de cuisine*.

"Speaking of juicy news," said Lawrence, leaning towards Molly, "what in the world is going on, with Castillacois dropping dead every five minutes! Is there some terrible infection sweeping the village?"

"I spoke to Florian. No infection. In fact, none of them had the same cause."

"Well, I'm not used to this galloping death rate and it's unsettling, don't you agree? *Four* villagers have died in two weeks. All on Sundays, I'll point out, and I don't begin to understand what the Lord is doing there and what that means. That's your department. But I'll tell you this: when Sunday rolls around this week, I'm going to be in bed early, covers pulled up to my chin and as far from trouble as I can get. Sober as a judge."

"Always wondered about that. Are judges especially sober? I would think not."

"*Molly.*"

"What?"

"Has the impending baby scrambled your senses? We have a veritable *stack* of dead people and you are leaning back in your chair, relaxed as can be. Not tapping your finger on something like you're the drummer for the Rolling Stones. Not looking off into the middle distance with that *cogitating* expression your friends know and love. You—you don't appear to be taking the reins in your usual fashion!"

Molly just smiled and patted her belly. "I'm not so fussed about the—as you rather callously put it—the *stack* of dead people."

"Well, why in the world not? I—and many others in the village as well, as you must realize—have come to depend on you. Just because you're having a baby doesn't mean you can just up and quit your job. There *are* such things as working mothers, you know."

She laughed again.

"I've never seen this side of you," he said, and he did not sound enchanted by it. "I'm not sure who you're laughing at, me or yourself," he said, tracing his fingers around the edge of his napkin, over and over.

"Both? Look, just this morning, as I told you, I went to see Florian—for the second time, mind you—after Matthias texted me about death number four. I figured the village would be leaping to conclusions and I wanted to get an idea about what was going on. Not that I had anything in mind. Do you? Have you been watching too much

TV and got an idea about a serial killer running around Castillac?"

Lawrence shrugged. "It's not that *I* pretend to know. But I don't think wanting some reassurance that there's no murder going on is horribly misplaced. There *has* been a murder or two in the village, you know. It's not *unthinkable*, Molly."

Molly nodded. "True enough. But serial killers are very rare, as I'm sure I've mentioned before. And they almost always have a clear and distinctive *modus operandi*—they kill the same way, have victims with something in common, often some sort of ritual..."

"And is this what you found in Aix-en-Provence?" said Lawrence.

"Well, okay, not exactly. But that was quite an unusual case."

"Exactly the point," said Lawrence. "*All* cases are unique, unusual in their way, am I right? Since when do you follow such conventional thinking, to assume that if a cluster of deaths do not tick every box on a list of commonalities, a serial killer is impossible? Those things you mention are only commonalities, Molly, *likelihoods*—not requirements. As you well know, since you yourself taught this truth to me."

With a sigh, Molly looked out of the window, distracted first by a mother pushing a stroller and then a teenaged boy on a skateboard. A long moment passed. Pascal brought a ruby-colored glass of Malbec for Lawrence and a glass of orange juice for Molly.

"Well, you are in a lecturing mood today," she said at last. "I just…I don't feel like thinking about murder right now. There is nothing that makes me believe these four people died in any way but in the natural course of things. I want to plan for the baby, hang out with Luka, have a normal, everyday, non-dangerous, unthreatening life. It would be different if I felt we were in danger—but I don't. After talking to Florian and hearing the causes of death—they're all different, and not a single one was violent in the least—I think the likelihood of a serial killer being responsible approaches zero. I would bet anything on that."

"*Anything?*"

Molly shrugged, not interested in any actual betting.

Lawrence fidgeted with his napkin some more. Then he spoke softly and Molly could hear the emotion in his voice. "Chérie, it's just…perhaps this is infantile of us, but the village depends on you to keep us safe. I know you sort of backed into this role, you didn't exactly come looking for it. But you have it and there's no un-having it, to coin an awkward phrase. There is a lot of stress in the world just now, people are losing their homes, going bankrupt, being put out on the street. Just turn on the television and you see tragedy everywhere. Everyone, even here in little out-of-the-way Castillac, is unsettled and worried about the future —the *near* future."

"I am hardly in any position to change any of that."

"You aren't going to set the fraudulent banks to rights, we can agree on that much. But if all that global stress and tension has contributed to someone here in Castillac going off the deep end— and if all four deaths are *not* natural—then yes, Molly Sutton, you *can* change that. And saying you're not in the mood right now, well, please excuse me for flying in so low—but I think you're going to have to step up and deal with it, whether you want to or not."

PAUL-HENRI MANSOUR, junior officer of the Castillac gendarmerie, was doing what he spent most of his working life doing: walking the streets of the village, eyes and ears open, watching and listening for trouble or any opportunity for making himself useful. So far, on that Tuesday, there had been no runaway dogs, no sufferers from dementia wandering the streets, no shoplifters, drunkards, scribblers of graffiti—not so much as a parking violation. He strolled with his hands clasped behind his back, nose in the air, enjoying the cooler weather, and thinking about a silk scarf he was considering buying that cost far more than he should be willing to pay, yet he wanted it badly and could not let the idea of it go.

After reaching the south end of the village and turning back, heading north on a different street, he realized his attention had been so taken up trying to decide between the maroon and the navy that he was not actually seeing anything in front of him. He might have strolled right past a serial killer doing a deed and missed him completely.

Serial killers being on Paul-Henri's mind lately, what with villagers dropping dead it seemed like every five minutes. Like many men, he had an interior fantasy life that involved being a sudden and unexpected hero, and nabbing a serial killer fit neatly with that.

But consciously, when he really thought about it? He wasn't so sure. Florian Nagrand had reassured him that the recent deaths were as natural as could be, and really, who in his right mind could come up with a reason to kill victim number four, a well-liked man who was a hundred and four years old?

But at the same time—who would say a serial killer was in his right mind?

With a sense of satisfaction Paul-Henri decided the matter was not yet settled. One by one he contemplated the newly deceased, trying to see a pattern, a motive, a reason.

Two women, one late middle-aged and one older.

Two men, one older and one very much older.

One Brit, three French.

One visitor, three locals.

In his mind, Paul-Henri saw these statements written inside circles—but the circles, as far as he could see, did not intersect. He went over it all again. Saw nothing.

It's just the kind of situation Molly Sutton delights in. Let's hope that baby on the way keeps her busy and well out of it, he thought with a pang of competitive jealousy as he entered the gendarmerie with nothing at all to report.

7

"Oh, hello there," said Molly as Ben came inside the kitchen of La Baraque, where she was taking out some wine glasses. "I just invited Rolanda over for a drink. Tell me about your day! I feel like I haven't seen you in an age."

"It's been four whole hours," said Ben, deadpan.

Molly went for a hug and leaned her face on his neck. "We haven't even been married a year," she said. "The thrill's not gone."

In his mind Ben heard the opening notes of B.B. King's song, which he knew was one of Molly's favorites.

A light tap on the French door of the terrace.

"Rolanda! Come on in, let me introduce you to

Ben." There were handshakes and then cheek-kisses and Rolanda took a glass of the Cabernet Sauvignon Molly poured.

"I might not finish it," said Rolanda. "I'm sure it's delicious! But I've been feeling a little under the weather."

"Oh no! What's been wrong? Is there anything we can do?"

Rolanda waved a hand in the air. "Oh no, I'm sure it's just...you know how it is, traveling can be so difficult sometimes. My flight was late so I had to sit in the airport for hour after hour, and then—well, I don't need to go through the whole trip point by point, you know what I mean, I'm sure. Probably I just need a day to rest after all of that."

"Certainly," said Ben. "We are fond of rest here at La Baraque."

"Seriously, the less exciting the better, as far as we're concerned."

Ben snorted.

"In some ways the worst part was all the televisions in the airport, constantly spewing doom and gloom. Next time I will bring earplugs because there was just no escaping it."

Molly took a moment. She didn't look at the news every day or even close to it, but she understood that the world as they knew it, in that precarious moment of October 2008, might turn out to look quite a bit different going forward, and not —to put it mildly—an improvement.

※

"Sorry for dropping by unannounced," Frances said, as she staggered inside La Baraque as though her legs were about to give out beneath her.

"Frances, please, come on in!"

"I haven't slept in...I don't remember what sleep even *is*."

Baby Luka let out a squall that actually rattled the old panes in the windows.

"Oh my," said Molly. "Let me take her?"

Frances began the complicated unbuckling of the carrier, lifted out the screaming baby, and handed her over. Then she walked to the sofa and lay down, putting a pillow over her head.

Rolanda complimented the baby, thanked Molly for the wine, and headed back to the pigeonnier.

Molly let the carrier drop to the floor and cradled Luka in her arms. She couldn't help it—even after holding her countless times—she still got a little *verklempt* at the sight of that little face. Which at the moment was scrunched up and screeching, wet with tears.

"Any idea what's bothering her?" said Molly, mostly unperturbed by the hollering.

"Probably a belly ache. Which means, since all she does is nurse, that I ate something she doesn't like. And apparently there are plenty of things she does not like, because almost every day at this time —I swear she waits for Nico to go to work—she starts up with the howling and nothing—*nothing*—I do seems to help."

Molly walked back and forth, jostling Luka in her arms and softly singing nonsense into her ear. In about five minutes, the baby was quiet. Then sound asleep.

When it got quiet, Frances came out from under the pillow and sat up. "How in the world did you do that?"

Molly shrugged. "I'm not positive, but I think the jiggling might have helped. I was sort of rough, like we were riding in a carriage going over a really bad road."

"Are you a baby whisperer?" asked Frances, eyes wide. "And let me just say for the hundredth time —I still can't believe you're pregnant. I know it's totally selfish but your pregnancy is pretty much the best thing that could've happened to me."

Molly laughed, understanding just what her friend meant. "I know, I feel the same. It's been four months and it still doesn't seem real to me half the time." She gave sleeping Luka a kiss on the head, still rocking from side to side, but more gently.

"Killer-catcher, baby-whisperer. That's quite a resume you've got there, Molls."

"I did a lot of babysitting before going to college."

"I remember that, actually. I kept inviting you to parties, and you wouldn't come because of some job. You're going to be genius at motherhood. Obviously!"

"I needed the money. But also really enjoyed the work. Okay, now what should we do? She's out cold but I don't have a crib set up or anything."

"Oh, you can just put her on a bed," said Frances. "She can't locomote yet," and somehow that fact struck them both as utterly hilarious and they laughed and laughed, eventually waking Luka again. She did not cry but looked quizzically from one to the other.

"So...don't answer this question if you don't feel like it," said Molly. "But how are you doing? A new baby is a lot, as I don't have to tell you. And I know you didn't exactly sign up for it—and so I just want to check in and see if you need anything?"

"How about around the clock nannies?"

Molly smiled. "The sleep deprivation is the

worst. At least that's what all the moms I used to work for told me."

"Emotional stability isn't easy to come by for me in the best of times. But on three hours sleep? Holy hell. You better pack in all the murder investigations you can before that baby comes, because afterwards, believe me, your brain is going to have more holes than a block of Emmenthaler."

"Mm."

"So...what about you? Have you been wondering about—what is it, three deaths in the village recently?"

"Four. And no, I'm not." Molly gave a Mona Lisa smile, which Frances noted but did not comment on.

The rest of the evening passed with the fascinating conversation typical of new and expectant mothers everywhere, covering all bodily excretions in deep detail. They had a few fond laughs at Nico's expense since the role of father was as much of a shock to him as motherhood was to Frances. There was not a single additional mention of death.

Which was exactly how Molly wanted it.

8

The shouting coming from the little house rented by Delphine Bardot was enough to make the neighbors stick their heads out of their windows to see what was going on.

But there was nothing to see, since the source of that noise, Daisy Bardot, was not on the street —or in their living rooms, which is how it sounded —but in Delphine's kitchen. The sound was barely dulled by the thin walls of the house.

"Just tell me, dear Maman, just how am I supposed to grow up to be a competent adult when my parents made such a mess of everything? That's how everyone learns, you know, from their parents. And I guess I just had all the luck to strike out twice."

Delphine took a deep breath before answering, trying to find some words that would not further inflame her daughter. "Sweetheart, I'm not going to try to defend myself. I know I made mistakes. Some big ones. But I have to protest against calling your father a strikeout. If I even understand what that means."

"What do you want to stick up for him for? It's not like you had this sweet, loving relationship."

"He didn't cheat on me. Or hit me."

"That's a low bar, Maman. A *really* low bar. *Merde*. You just don't get it. I'll tell you exactly why he's a strikeout. It doesn't really have much to do with you or how he did or didn't treat you. Not everything is about you, you know."

Delphine bowed her head. She remembered taking Daisy to Central Park, in Manhattan, and how the little girl had loved running through the Sheep's Meadow, back and forth, with endless energy and joy.

Daisy tucked her dyed-black hair behind her ears, then gathered it into a ponytail with an elastic. She picked up a chef's knife from the kitchen table and ran it lightly down her forearm, shaving the hair off. She shook her head, making the ponytail bounce. "What did Daddy *do* with his life?" she said. "He worked his ass off, that's what. And that's *it*, that was his life, from beginning to end. Always at the office. Never home, never with us."

"Is that fair? He—"

"Oh, come on. See reality for once! He chose—he was an *adult*, right? It's not as though his life just happened to him and he had no say in the matter, made no decisions about it. He chose what were the most important things to him to dedicate his life to, and those two things were making money and avoiding other people. That includes *us*, Maman. And the icing on the cake—the crazy irony—after all those years chasing money, his partner cheated him out of it, leaving us practically destitute. Actually, maybe it's not irony. Maybe it's payback."

"It wasn't—"

"It *was!*" Daisy shouted. Delphine cringed. "Just face it! You picked the worst man to marry in all of New York!"

Delphine smiled, a wan sort of smile. "Could that be just a slight exaggeration?"

"No it is not!" shouted Daisy.

"Will you please, for the love of God, keep your voice down?" Delphine snapped. Then she tried to soften her voice. "It's not that I don't want to hear what you have to say. But do the neighbors and anyone walking down the street have to hear it too? This is not New York, after all."

Daisy glared. Her nostrils flared as though she were a cartoon bull being flashed with a red cape. Slowly she ran the knife along her cheek. She smiled.

She muttered something Delphine did not quite catch but guessed (correctly) was vulgar. Then her daughter tossed the knife on the table and was out the door, letting it bang behind her. She took off running down the street, the eyes of most of the neighbors following her progress.

DELPHINE SPENT the rest of the day in seclusion. Milo texted her several times but she did not answer, even knowing that would infuriate him. She needed time to think without anyone intruding—though she worried about Daisy: where she was, what she might be doing, and wished for her to come home.

Delphine's body felt achy and she took a long hot bath. She put rosemary oil in her hair and several serums on her face, for a long time looking at herself in the mirror, wondering about history and truth and age and how a person can ever know anything at all for sure.

Like watching a movie that was captivating but not exactly inspiring, she saw the story of her marriage unfold as she lay in the tub. Saw her husband when she first met him, remembered how lucky she felt to have found this ambitious Frenchman in New York, who seemed so smitten with her. Thought of the rambling, expensive apartment where they lived, all the credit cards he had given her to use while giving nothing of himself—not his time, or attention, or really anything at all...except for all that money.

She felt the loneliness of his absence, even while in the same room with him.

Why had she not felt angry about that when it was happening? Why did it take her daughter spelling it out for Delphine to fully grasp the reality of how it had been?

Some part of her wanted to sink under the water in the tub and stay there. That part was drawn to the soft promise of escape, of an end to anxiety, of oblivion.

Daisy was right about Milo, too; it didn't take a rocket scientist to see that.

She allowed herself to sink deep into self-pity, remembering the terrible treatment she had received from that first serious boyfriend, way back in high school...how had she turned into a perennial victim? This was not who she was, deep down, or who she wanted to be.

At last, when it was bedtime, Delphine texted

Daisy to ask where she was, knowing it would annoy her but firm in her parental right since her daughter was still young enough to live at home.

No response.

Delphine tried to tell herself she was letting her imagination run away with her, but she felt... something ominous. Something not right. Something...threatening.

Had it been a mistake to try to come home again? It had seemed less scary than trying to make a go of it in New York City. But she and Daisy needed an income, and what jobs were they going to find in little old Castillac? Was it only that anxiety that was troubling her, or something else?

When she was in her nightgown and just climbing into her twin bed, Delphine heard a baby crying—it sounded like it was right outside her bedroom window, in the little alley. She did not jump up and go outside to see what was going on. Of course she had an instantaneous response to help—*a baby was in trouble and needed her!*—but she knelt on the bed for a long moment, frozen.

A current of fear went through her and she was in the grip of it even though she had no understanding of where it was coming from.

Maybe she had misunderstood, maybe it was just a cat in heat?

She lay down on the bed and looked out of

the window. She could still hear the baby crying, and she tried to look up and down the alley, but it was a cloudy night with no moon and she couldn't see much of anything. No baby, no basket, or anything else that might contain a baby.

Just a street in darkness.

She moved away from the window and lay in bed trembling. The crying stopped abruptly and Delphine heard nothing else, just the silence of night on a back alley in a small village.

As she lay in bed, Delphine worried more and more about that baby. What if it had stopped crying because it was too exhausted to cry anymore and was on the brink of death?

She called the gendarmerie. Paul-Henri lived only a few blocks from Delphine and when he got the call, he quickly put on his uniform and jogged over to see what was going on.

"The Chief asked me to check things out, make sure you were all right," he said, out of breath, when Delphine opened the door.

"You're going to think I'm silly," she said quietly.

"Come on now, tell me what the problem is."

He started to pat her shoulder but stopped himself and let the hand drop awkwardly.

"There was a baby," she said.

Paul-Henri waited. Delphine tightened the sash to her bathrobe, her head down.

"Baby? Whose baby? Where?"

"In the alley. I mean—there was the sound of a baby. Crying. But I couldn't see anything."

Paul-Henri felt a flash of disappointment. "A baby crying? That's it?"

"Well…I…maybe my imagination…I just wondered…"

Paul-Henri went ahead and put his hand on her shoulder, and felt her relax just a little.

"I thought…I had the sudden thought that maybe someone was trying to lure me outside. Like there wasn't an actual baby, it was a recording. Sort of like…bait."

Paul-Henri nodded solemnly as though chewing this over with much concern. "Not a real baby," he said finally.

"I'm being silly."

"No, surely not. Shall I go have a look around? Would that give you some reassurance?"

Delphine nodded.

Where was Daisy? It wasn't as though Castillac had clubs open late at night, or even a bar, not on a Wednesday.

"Where do you feel safest?" asked Paul-Henri. "The bedroom? Go in there. Wait—lock the door after me first, then go in the bedroom. I'm going to walk all around the house and down the alley, and see what I can see. Do any of your neighbors have a baby?"

"Not that I know of," said Delphine, barely louder than a whisper.

He stepped outside and waited to hear the lock turn before moving away. He stood back from the house and observed. Then he walked to the alley, stopping to look in both directions, as well as up to the second-floor balcony of a house on the other side, the rooftops, the garages. He walked slowly down the alley, two blocks, and then back again.

Paul-Henri took the concerns of his constituency seriously. He was able to put aside his own personal judgment and address the person's problem wholeheartedly. No alley and perimeter of a house had been searched more thoroughly.

9

The next morning, Paul-Henri came to the gendarmerie to make his report to Chief Charlot before going about his market day rounds.

"Ah, that Delphine Bardot—she's a nervous one," he said, shrugging his shoulders. "I checked the alleyway, the street, the house—there was nothing out of place. You know Delphine has always been...sensitive."

"I shouldn't need to point out that sensitivity is not a character defect, as you seem to be implying. It can be very useful. In collecting evidence, for example."

Paul-Henri hung his head. "All I can report is that I saw no baby, heard no baby, and the streets were quiet as a tomb."

"Unfortunate turn of phrase," said the Chief, turning away to look at her computer. "Go by there again tonight, at around the same time. No need to knock on Delphine's door or let her know you are coming. Do a thorough check."

Paul-Henri suppressed a sigh. If only there *had* been an abandoned baby, he thought. The night would have been so much more exciting.

※

ALBERTINE DUPONT WAS out walking that Saturday night, as she was every night. On rue Balzac, some trash left over from the market was in the gutter—only some pieces of cardboard and vegetable scraps—and she picked them up and put them in a garbage bin, muttering under her breath about people who didn't follow the rules and how much she disliked people who didn't follow the rules.

She went in a pattern on her nightly walks, a spiraling route that began wide and narrowed block by block until she reached her apartment and went back inside. For the most part, at that late hour, in the dark with the air cooling down quickly, she encountered few other villagers. Which was just how she liked it.

As she went down rue Jules Michelet, Albertine appeared to be lost in thought, walking quickly, rapidly tapping her fingers on the sides of her thighs.

She reached Delphine's house and stopped. She lifted her nose in the air and sniffed. Her fingers tapped even more quickly. She sniffed again.

"Bonsoir, Albertine," said Paul-Henri, appearing from the shadows.

She startled violently. "Bonsoir," she murmured, looking down at the pavement.

"I wonder if you happened to be on this street last night?"

Albertine shook her head.

"Hm. There was a report of a crying baby. Just wondering if you knew anything about that."

Albertine shook her head harder.

"All right then," said Paul-Henri. "Don't stay out too late," he added, thinking of the serial killer and how he might valiantly come to Albertine's rescue if the killer stepped out from the alley and tried something. His daydream went so far as to see himself accepting a medal of honor that Chief Charlot put around his neck to the wild applause of the entire village.

10

Florence had been the housekeeper at a manor house on the south end of Castillac for over twenty years. She shopped for food and brought it to the house twice a week, and cleaned with a dedicated fury that depended on great vats of vinegar, lemons, heaps of rags, and several powerful machines. Florence did not feel this work was drudgery and she performed it to a very high standard.

The owner of the house, Ginette Duchamps, had never married and did not socialize—except with Florence—whom she peppered with questions each morning as soon as Florence came through the back door into the kitchen and set about her work.

"Has anyone else died?" was the first question Madame Duchamps had asked for the last several weeks. Florence, it must be said, was equally interested in the deaths in the village, equally frightened, and also very curious about whether the deaths were natural or not.

"Maybe we're too suspicious," Madame Duchamps had said at first. "But maybe not. We in Castillac know a thing or two about murder, after all, we've seen it before. And I can't help thinking that Chief Charlot is just sitting on her hands while the village is decimated. Decimated!" Madame Duchamps had said on Friday. Florence had agreed with her, as she always did (on the principle that agreeing with your employer was only common sense), but this time she meant it.

Florence had said that she was positive Molly Sutton was working the case—everyone knew her record—Sutton was a confirmed genius when it came to murder—and all she and Madame Duchamps had to do was lock the doors, sit back, and wait for Molly to nail the perpetrator. Madame Duchamps had seemed only mildly comforted by this; she had never met this Molly Sutton and it was difficult to feel confident about putting her life in this unknown woman's hands, and a foreigner to boot.

This exchange was going through Florence's

mind as she came to the back door that Monday morning. She slipped the key into the lock, approving that Madame Duchamps had remembered to lock up, since it had not been her habit.

On Mondays especially, Madame Duchamps was always waiting for her in the kitchen. Ready with a pile of questions and observations that she had built up over the weekend with no one to share them with.

But on that Monday, she was not in the kitchen.

Or the pantry. Or the study. Or anywhere downstairs.

Florence did not call out because Madame Duchamps did not approve of shouting in the house. (Or anywhere.)

Without making any preparations for her work, Florence went upstairs and looked in each room—four bedrooms on the first floor, two with ensuite bathrooms, though Madame Duchamps never had guests.

On the landing of the stairs she cocked her head to listen. She could hear some birds arguing outside. The lowing of a cow from the farm next door. A creak somewhere above, which sounded to Florence more like the usual sighing of the house than anyone walking—but she went up to the second floor to investigate, her heart in her throat.

Two more bedrooms. Florence made a mental note to come back and dust the bedposts, which had some carved curlicues that held the dust and needed extra attention.

In the bathroom between the two bedrooms, Florence found Madame Duchamps sitting on a bathmat, slumped against the side of the imposing tub that no one ever used.

Florence gasped. She reached for her phone but even as she hurriedly called the emergency number, she could see that no amount of hurrying was going to help Madame Duchamps now.

It was too late for that.

II

11

The morning was brisk and Molly decided to take a good long walk and stretch her legs. Ben had gotten up early and taken off for his latest job; she had a second cup of coffee standing in the kitchen before heading out, Bobo at her side.

At her side for a moment, anyway—soon the dog streaked ahead, leapt over the ditch, disappeared into the forest, yipped at something she found, streaked back across the road, and was swallowed up by the ferns, which were turning brown as they did in October.

"You're exhausting just to watch," Molly said, peering into the ferns to see where the dog had gone.

Molly's mind was clear. Unusually relaxed. She

had nothing to do but take care of herself and let her baby grow—that was all. Her usual restlessness was nearly gone. The fact of the baby was so momentous, so deeply wished for, that it took up almost all of her attention as well as mental and emotional energy.

She walked and walked, simply letting her gaze fall on this tree or that shed, not thinking about anything in particular but simply adrift in the pleasure of moving her legs and not having a single thing on her plate that she needed to worry about or accomplish.

The road wound gently through the countryside; there were few cars or people to be seen. A tractor passed by and the farmer waved at Molly and she waved back though she did not recognize him.

She walked several more kilometers before feeling a pang of hunger. She had reached a small farm and she leaned on the fence for a moment, looking around. A herd of cream-colored Charolais eating hay. A farm dog running around with the clear sense that he was the boss of all proceedings. Molly thought she heard some goats but could not see any. It was hilly and she could see the pasture stretching up behind the barn. What a wonderful change it has been, she thought, to buy my food from farms instead of supermarkets.

She turned back towards home, considering that she might have walked too far. Just then, her phone buzzed in her pocket and she pulled it out, expecting Ben to be sending an update on the job he was working.

But the text was from Matthias.

#5 Ginette Duchamps

Molly shook her head as though to refuse the text, to make it wrong. She sighed and looked back at the cows, tried to absorb their contented complacency.

Five *is* rather a lot, she thought. But then shook her head again. She set off down the road towards home, one hand patting her belly that was starting to get noticeably bigger, and focused on the birdsong and the trees whose leaves were turning color but not yet falling. There was a chilly breeze and she focused on that too. And the feel of her feet pressing into the road with each step, and the brightness of the sun.

She refused to think about death, or Ginette Duchamps, or any of the others. Her attention—as it should be, she thought with some force—was on the beauty of the natural world and on her baby.

Matthias should find someone else to pester.

People die. There's no escaping it. This pressure she felt—it was like the villagers wanted her to magically take death off the table, as though they could all live forever. She shrugged and headed for home, thinking about lunch.

12

"Well, aren't you blooming!" said Frances, as Molly came into Chez Papa grinning her head off. "Did you just win the lottery?"

"I'd say so," said Molly, still grinning and patting her belly. "Bonjour, Mademoiselle," she added, giving Luka a kiss on the head as she dozed in the baby carrier.

Nico slid a glass of fresh orange juice in front of Molly.

"Merci, Nico. I do miss my kirs—not that I'm complaining!" Which led Molly and Frances into a long conversation about nursing and alcohol while Nico went to the other end of the bar to talk about soccer with an old schoolmate.

After exhausting that topic, Molly spun around

85

on her stool just in time to see Gilbert Renaud come sauntering into the bistro and slide into a banquette next to his mother, who was having lunch with Delphine Bardot. Young Gilbert had been instrumental in solving a case a few years before, but Molly had barely seen him since.

Molly hopped off the stool to go say hello. "Gilbert!" She leaned in for cheek kisses. "I haven't seen you in an *age!* Bonjour, Madame Renaud, bonjour Delphine, we haven't met," she added.

The two women nodded and said bonjour, but it was plain that neither welcomed Molly's interruption. "Well, I'll leave you to it," Molly said, winking at Gilbert. "Come see me sometime, if you're looking for something to do," she said to the boy, knowing that his mother was very strict and did not allow him much freedom.

And also knowing that she, Molly, had never been on Madame Renaud's list of approved persons, even though she had more or less saved Gilbert's life during that long-ago case.

"Another one of your teenage *dévotés?*" said Frances, nodding at Gilbert, who was slumped down in the banquette looking like he wished a hole would open in the floor and swallow him right up.

"He's a cutie," said Molly. She leaned in to whisper, "...but his mother will barely let him out of her sight. *So* over-protective. That's not going to happen to us, is it?"

"I plan to keep Luka in this baby carrier until she's old enough to vote."

"Understood." Molly laughed and looked back over to the banquette. "Do you happen to know Madame Renaud's first name? There's something a little forbidding about her, *n'est-ce pas?* I just realized I've known her for several years and never even imagined using her first name. I don't even know what it is."

"Beats me," said Frances. She took hold of Luka's little feet and squeezed them.

"I wonder how Madame Renaud and Delphine know each other."

"What's to wonder? Seems to me everybody in the village knows everybody else."

"Sure, but that doesn't mean they're friends. Just...seems like an odd couple, is all I'm saying." Molly glanced over to the banquette once again and saw Madame Renaud shaking her head forcefully, and Gilbert sinking even farther down so that his head was barely above the table.

Madame Renaud is not going to stand for that, Molly thought, and in the next instant Madame Renaud did in fact give Gilbert an elbow to the ribs and lean over to say something in his ear, and the boy struggled back upright with an expression as though someone were yanking his fingernails out with pliers.

The door opened, letting in a cool breeze, and Molly watched Albertine come inside and go to a table along the wall, across the room from Madame Renaud and Delphine. Molly had seen Albertine around, from time to time, but they had never been introduced.

"Weirdo," said Frances, simply and without judgment.

Molly shrugged.

Albertine sat with her shoulders pulled way down, a scarf knotted around her neck. She stroked the fringe on the scarf while scowling at the banquette where Delphine and Madame Renaud were talking intently.

"You've met her?" Molly asked.

"Albertine? Nah. Not really. She comes in here sometimes. She's...she's angry a lot. I get the feeling she's chock-full of resentments."

"Mm," said Molly. "A lot of people are. And perhaps—often enough—not without reason."

　　　　　　　　　🐌

"GILBERT, here's some money, trot over to the *épicerie*, will you, and get us two cans of beans and some dishwashing soap?"

Gilbert started to ask what kind of beans, but he was a perceptive lad and he understood that his mother wanted to be alone with Delphine and this trip to the épicerie was just an excuse. So he decided to buy himself some candy and not worry too much about the beans.

The door slammed behind him and Chez Papa was suddenly quiet.

"Look," said Delphine, "just to be really clear—there's no hard feelings, okay?"

"Ssh! Good heavens, keep your voice down," hissed Madame Renaud. She tucked her wavy hair behind her ears, gnawing on her lower lip. "If there's one thing I know, keeping your business private is more important than ever."

"Oh please, don't be so dramatic. Surely—"

"Delphine! I'm asking you—for my son's sake, if nothing else—*please* keep this whole thing to yourself. It's really nobody else's business, you certainly must agree to that at least? What good would come of giving the whole village one more thing to gossip about?"

Delphine cocked her head and observed the other woman. She was unused to being in the power position, in which someone else was begging her to do—or not do—something.

Like nearly anyone would—she rather enjoyed it.

"I don't know," Delphine said slowly, just to prolong the feeling, and also—just a bit—to torture Madame Renaud, since she did not like her. Delphine meant it when she said there were no hard feelings—but that didn't mean her feelings towards Madame Renaud were warm. Or even tepid.

For one thing—why did Madame Renaud insist that everyone call her "Madame"? She was around Delphine's age, not some village elder who deserved formality and deference. In the moment, Delphine couldn't even remember her first name. Was it Heloise? Hélène? Huguette? Did it even begin with an H?

"I realize I am in no position to ask," said Madame Renaud, for once deferential herself, startling Delphine out of her thoughts. "But it would mean quite a lot to me if you would tell me how you found out."

Delphine sat back with a Mona Lisa smile. This was far more enjoyable than she had anticipated it would be. She shrugged and looked towards the door as if thinking about leaving.

"Wait!" said Madame Renaud, whose first name was Cataline. "I know you don't owe me anything. And you were long gone when all this happened—you had been in New York City for years, you were married with children of your own!"

Delphine nodded slowly. She shrugged again.

"May I ask if those years were…fulfilling? Did you like your life there?"

"We were rich. On balance, I would say, if you have a choice? Rich is better."

Madame Renaud could not help allowing an eyeroll. "And what happened to the money?"

"That's none of your business."

"Exactly. Which is just what I say to you about the events of long ago. So long I barely remember it. And it is no one's business but mine. And perhaps Gilbert's, but he is too young to be involved in any of this, and so I beg—yes, *beg*—you to keep quiet about it."

"We'll see," said Delphine. "Now, I have some errands to run so I'll say goodbye. Again—no hard feelings," she said, reaching her hand out for a limp handshake before hurrying out of Chez Papa and letting the door bang behind her.

Night was well underway. Moonless and cold. Daisy found herself—which was how it felt to her, as though she moved from one place to the next without conscious intention, and was surprised by where she ended up—in a stone house at the edge of the village, with some people she did not know.

You could call them unsavory characters: people who lived on the fringes of village life, disconnected, some addicted, short of money and anything to live for. Daisy was attracted to them because they were angry too. And because she felt that she was better than they were, though she did not ask herself on what evidence she made such a determination.

"Beer?" said a very thin young man with pale skin who was reclined on a ratty cushion taken from a long-gone sofa.

"Nah," said Daisy. She looked around the room. There was only one other woman there, and she was sitting in the lap of a man who appeared to be passed out, his head lolling back and body limp. "This is the truth of what humanity is," Daisy said, not to anyone is particular. "That's what I could never get my parents to understand. All they ever cared about is the external, the surface, what other people think."

"Where you from?" the thin man asked. "Can't place your accent."

Daisy narrowed her eyes. She dug into her jeans pocket and pulled out a fistful of euros. "What've you got," she asked him. "No needles."

The thin man laughed. "Go talk to Abbie," he said. "In the back." He waved his hand and then his head slumped back down and his eyes closed.

Daisy went to the back and found Abbie, paid for a handful of pills, swallowed several without water, and sat down to wait.

A short and thick man sat down beside her.

"Not looking for company," she said, glaring in her fiercest New Yorker way.

"Me neither," said the man.

"Get lost then."

"I'll sit where I like."

"Scram. I don't want you sitting there."

"Too bad."

Daisy felt rage boiling up from her belly, could feel the surge of it going into her chest and down her arms and legs, blazing hot and uncontrollable. She stood up and kicked the man in the ribs as hard as she could. He gasped and looked up at Daisy in shock.

And then she walked nonchalantly to the door of the little house and went outside, where she ran as fast as she could into an alleyway and the safety of shadows.

13

Delphine had come back to Castillac in part to reconnect with old friends. At least, that was what she told herself. But once she was back, Delphine had taken up with Milo and he had all her attention. One of the friends, Solange Forestier, had heard where Delphine was living, and decided to drop by to see her for the first time in decades.

The morning was cool and Solange wore an old leather jacket and a scarf. She moved quickly down the street because she was a fast walker—was known for it, teased about it—and so she arrived at Delphine's house quickly and rapped on the door.

No answer.

Solange called their mutual friend Marielle. "I thought you said Delphine was at 43 Malbec?"

"Bonjour to you too, Solange."

"Well, there's no answer."

"Maybe she's still asleep. As I was."

"You're sure it's the right address? I've got some things to talk to her about."

"I'm sure a lot of us do. There's years and years of catching up to do."

"I mean some serious things."

"Right," said Marielle, rolling her eyes. "I'm going back to sleep, talk to you later."

Solange knocked on the door again, really banging on it. She cocked her ear but heard no sound coming from inside. She tried the doorknob; it turned. Solange slipped inside.

"Coo-coo!" she called. The kitchen was messy—crumbs littering the table and a pile of dirty pots in the sink.

She walked into the small living room. "Hey Delphine! Blast from the past here to say hello!"

No answer.

Solange noticed a funny feeling in her stomach. Like literal butterflies fluttering there, beating their wings against her insides.

She came to a bedroom door that was ajar, and pushed it open.

It did not take any medical knowledge to see that her old friend, who lay tangled in the sheets on her back, eyes open—had passed on to the next world.

"*Merde*," muttered Solange, shaking her head.

⁂

FLORIAN AND MATTHIAS did not especially like each other, but they worked very well together. Having received the call from the gendarmerie, they went quickly to the white van of the coroner's office and drove the short distance to the house on rue Malbec where Delphine Bardot had been living with her daughter.

Solange had waited for them, feeling a need to tell the story of her discovery of her friend, and also because leaving the body alone just didn't feel right.

"What in hell is going on," she said to Florian, not expecting any kind of satisfactory answer. "People are dropping dead practically every day now."

"Not my department," he said, bending over Delphine to make a first inspection. "Is this exactly how she was? You haven't moved her or touched anything on the bed?"

"Of course not," said Solange.

Matthias made a discreet eyeroll at Florian's question, which Solange was pleased to see.

"Was anyone else here? What about Delphine's daughter?"

"Oh! I haven't looked."

Matthias left the bedroom and walked two steps to the other bedroom. The door was shut but not locked and he opened it and looked inside. An unmade bed, the smell of cheap perfume, a pile of clothes on the floor. But no Daisy.

"Other bedroom is empty."

"Well, let's see, it's not even seven o'clock. What are the odds that the daughter got up early and is out doing something healthful?" said Florian.

"Is this your department?" asked Matthias.

Florian shot him a look and turned his attention back to the body. "Set up the stretcher, if you don't mind," he said.

Solange felt in the way and asked if they needed her for anything else.

"You'll be contacted by the gendarmerie, most likely," said Florian. "Of course at this stage I cannot say anything about the cause of death."

"Do you think—I mean, Delphine wasn't old. Or sick, that I heard of," said Solange.

Florian shrugged. He was an expressive shrugger. The message was: who knows.

14

The news of Delphine's death traveled quickly through Castillac, as most news did. It caught up with Milo Clavel as he was having breakfast at the Café de la Place, which he could not afford, being flat broke.

Pascal heard it from Solange as she went by on her way to work; he hesitated about telling Milo, thinking—correctly—that Milo was unpredictable and might cause a scene. But Pascal did not think it was right not to tell him, and so, as sympathetically as he could, that is what he did.

At first Milo showed no sign of comprehending what Pascal had said.

"Surely you have oatmeal on the menu? I know it's not your standard croissant and orange juice, but this is a restaurant for God's sake," Milo said. "I have a yen for oatmeal this morning."

"Did you hear what I just said? Delphine—"

"Delphine, Delphine, Delphine. It's always something with her, know what I mean? Women! Sometimes I—wait, what?"

Pascal blinked at him, waiting.

"Did you just tell me she's...*dead?*"

Pascal nodded. He put a hand on Milo's thin shoulder. Milo looked at Pascal's hand with distaste, then jumped up from his chair.

"What is this, some kind of prank? I never liked you, Pascal. And now here is proof that I was right."

Pascal stepped back, face frozen. "Milo..."

In a flash, Milo's expression went from bravado to collapse. "She was my love," moaned Milo, dropping back into the chair.

Pascal stepped back some more.

"She was the best thing that ever happened to me," Milo said, taking his head out of his hands and sipping his coffee.

Pascal kept walking backwards until he was all the way to the swinging door to the kitchen, which he backed through.

"Maman," he said with some urgency. "I told the news to Milo. And I don't know, maybe I'm overreacting. But he seems...unstable. I'm not sure what he's going to do next, and I wish he were out of the café."

Pascal's mother was unperturbed and continued to assemble the *daube* for the lunch special. "Take him an orange juice on the house," she said. "And then leave him alone. He'll find his way out."

Her advice was good, as Pascal knew it would be. About ten minutes later he watched Milo, having glugged down the orange juice, lurch from his chair and out into the brisk day, blinking in the sun, and take off down the street in a hurry. Pascal started to wonder where he was going—but Pascal was the kind of man who took people as they were and did not spend any energy thinking about why they did what they did, and so the wondering did not last.

༄

WELL, he was no expert on these matters and never claimed to be, but Lapin was no idiot, he would say that much about himself. And what he was thinking that October morning, after hearing the news about Delphine—

Six is too many.

Six is way *way* over the line of reasonable.

The deaths were coming like clockwork, faster and faster now, and he, Lapin, was not going to simply sit back in his shop, twiddling his thumbs and worrying—he was going to do something about it.

I am a man of action, he said to himself, as he drove too fast to La Baraque and once there, leapt from his car without even shutting the car door and banged the knocker as hard as he could.

"What in the world," said Molly, opening the door and motioning for him to come inside. "Bonjour, Lapin. Do you have spiders in your underwear?"

"Is that some Americanism? Because I will tell you right now I am not in the mood."

"Actually I just made it up. Seemed a decent explanation for your—"

"Did you hear?"

"About what?"

"*Delphine Bardot.*"

"Yes," said Molly.

"And?"

"And what?"

"What are you going to do about it?"

"Would you like some coffee? Come sit down. Gather yourself."

"I am plenty *gathered*, for heaven's sake, Molly!" But he went to the living room and sat on the sofa across from the woodstove, which was not lit.

Molly bustled in the kitchen and in a few minutes brought out two steaming cups of coffee, Lapin's with cream and extra sugar. She sat next to her friend and put a hand on his arm as he took his coffee. "Look, Lapin. I know that for the last few years I've been on a tear, investigating any and everything that went on in the village, even when people didn't want me to."

"I never once said I didn't want you to."

"Thank you for that. I do appreciate it. But you know, things change. *I've* changed. I've got something else occupying my mind right now—life instead of death. And I'll tell you: I like life better. *Much* better." She patted her belly and grinned at him.

Lapin looked at her in disbelief. "Who *are* you? I mean, I'm very happy about your baby, don't get me wrong. Contentment is all well and good, no doubt. Babies are cute and all, yada yada yada. But you're...you're *Molly*. You're supposed to be restless and curious and when someone dies out of nowhere, you're *on the case*. And this? This is a case like nothing Castillac has ever seen. Six deaths in a matter of weeks, Molly! People—and by that I mean me—are *terrified*."

Molly shrugged. "Honestly, in my opinion? I think you can relax. I know, six does sound like a lot, I'll give you that. But math can be funny. Our minds desperately want to make patterns out of everything. We want regularity, we want predictability. One death in the village every few months—preferably someone ancient and ready to go—for a total of five or six a year, at most. And the same the following year, and the year after that. We want to know what's coming."

Lapin opened his mouth but Molly put a hand up and continued, "What I'm trying to tell you is that it just doesn't work that way. I totally understand that six makes people nervous. It's understandable. But that number is not, in *any* way, proof of anything. Fluctuations are normal, even if unsettling. So lean back, Lapin, enjoy your coffee, and tell me—are you involved in the estates of the newly passed on? Have you received anything interesting? I have a nursery to outfit so I'd be looking for—"

"I never in my life thought I would hear you be so callous," he said, setting his cup down and starting to get up.

"I don't mean to be—I'm only talking about the reasons for the deaths, not that I don't care about them. Of course I am sorry for their friends and family—doesn't that go without saying, between you and me? Were you friends with any of them?"

"I knew Delphine. Not intimately. But we did know each other."

"Condolences on your loss."

"Was that sarcastic?"

"Of course not. You are...quite touchy today, Lapin. Is something else bothering you?"

"Something *else?* Molly—" Lapin looked at her with his head cocked to one side. "You will think this rude of me but it appears that pregnancy has addled your brain."

Molly laughed, and the carefree sound of it, throaty and warm, made Lapin smile in spite of himself. "Like most of the world," he said, "I do not handle change well. So to see you go from a person who is obsessed—not too strong a word, I don't believe—with murder and injustice to a person who in the face of a village slaughter is intent on thinking about outfitting a nursery and some gobbledygook about math—well, it's more than I can take this morning."

Molly simply smiled a calm, beatific smile, which pushed Lapin right to the brink.

"Well, what does Madame Tessier think?" he said. Craftily.

A little spark flashed in Molly's mind. "Madame Tessier?"

"Of course she'll know everything there is to know about the victims."

"We don't know they're victims, Lapin. Unless

now we're considering any death to be victimization, which in my opinion is going a little far."

"Can't you at least have a coffee with Madame Tessier, just to…just to…do whatever it is the two of you do when you put your heads together? She lives on the same street as the first person who died, you know. She's going to have insight."

Molly smiled again. "If it makes you feel better? If I really believed someone had murdered those six people, I would—of course—be sniffing around to see what I could find out. But like I keep saying, I don't think that is the case. There is no evidence for it. People die, Lapin. It's what we do, every single one of us, eventually. And we don't get offered a calendar where we can choose the moment." She shrugged.

Lapin felt his blood pressure rising and rising.

Ben came in through the French door, back from his morning run. "Bonjour Lapin!" he said, coming over to kiss cheeks. "Has Molly got you scouting nursery furniture? Because we're—"

"Oh, stop it! Stop talking about the nursery furniture for God's sake!" Lapin cried, jumping up and putting his hands on top of his head. "What is the matter with you people? It's as though you've drunk some kind of potion that's changed your personalities entirely. I don't like it one bit! Good day to you!"

And with that, Lapin rushed out the front door, his delicious coffee only half-drunk.

"What's got him in such a state?" asked Ben.

"There's been a sixth," said Molly quietly. "Delphine Bardot."

"Oh."

"Do you think six is...too many?"

Ben shrugged. "We don't know."

Molly nodded. "Right. It's not proof of anything."

"Not proof. Could be, or not. We...don't know."

Molly nodded, chewing on her lip for the briefest moment, then she clapped her hands together and started talking about what to have for lunch.

15

They ate with enormous appetite, so focused on the food they barely spoke. Afterward, Molly surveyed the wreckage of the table on the terrace.

"I see your appetite is back," said Ben, deadpan as usual.

She laughed. "I could eat...*mountains* of food. I've never felt a hunger like this ever in my life, and you know I've always enjoyed my food rather a lot. But now? I feel like I could eat a mastodon. And the mastodon's entire family. With the deepest pleasure."

Ben laughed. "It's nice to see," he said, and then looked off over the meadow where Bobo could be spotted from time to time, bounding after some small creature. "And what about Lapin?"

"What about him? You know—and I say this with love—he's always had a bit of a scared bunny somewhere inside him."

Ben shrugged.

They sat in the sunshine, thinking their own thoughts.

"Six *is* a lot," said Ben.

Molly nodded. "What about dinner? Maybe I should do something a little ambitious? You have any particular yearnings?"

"October means stew to me."

"On it," said Molly, and leaned back and closed her eyes, face in the sun.

Neither made any move to get up, enjoying the lingering feeling of a good lunch with nothing too pressing to hurry off to.

"I've been thinking," said Ben.

Molly sat up.

"I don't want this to sound morbid, but perhaps it is."

"You're not going to be pushing me to investigate the deaths too?"

"No, no, that's not it at all. Though the deaths have made me think. People do die out of nowhere sometimes. It's not like everybody has the luxury of dying of old age, you know? There are accidents, infections, all kinds of—"

"You *are* morbid."

"It's just that I think, now that we're going to be parents, in order to be organized and conscientious, we should get our wills done. So that our child will be taken care of as best we can, just in case."

Molly was watching a bird hop from branch to branch.

"Do you agree? Should I call André and have him come over and we can get it set up?"

"I'm not opposed. But my understanding of French inheritance law is that if one spouse dies, the other spouse automatically inherits. And if both spouses die, the children automatically inherit. So do we really have any complications to worry about? It's not like we've got some massive pile of assets to protect. *Au contraire*."

"That is true. But it doesn't hurt to have our wishes spelled out. For instance, I don't know whether your not being French has any bearing on anything. And André might have some interesting advice on the tax part of it."

"Whatever, if you want," said Molly, who at that moment was much more interested in finding a crib than tax law.

"I know I usually ask you to come to the gendarmerie for these sorts of updates, but I wanted to stretch my legs. Hope you don't mind."

"Of course, of course, not at all," said Florian, gesturing to Chief Charlot to sit in the chair by his desk.

"Bonjour Matthias," she said, nodding in his direction. "All right. Now then." She pulled her uniform jacket down and smoothed her hair, wishing she were somewhere else. "As I don't have to tell you, the count is up to six deaths. Delphine was relatively young, had no prior health problems that I've heard about. Did you find otherwise?"

"Chief Charlot, with all due respect, we only picked up the body a few hours ago. The autopsy is slated for this afternoon."

"Then what are you doing, lounging around the office? Why don't you get to it!"

"We did not allow the autopsy to take precedence over lunch. As any civilized persons would not. It's not as though, at this point, as far as Delphine Bardot is concerned, there is any desperate hurry. In addition, I am training Matthias, which does slow the process, though I am pleased to report he is quite a quick study."

SEVEN CORPSES ALL IN A ROW

Matthias suppressed a smile at this unexpected compliment.

"*Six*," said Charlot.

"I am aware," said Florian.

"If there is anything—and I mean *any*thing—that seems the slightest, tiniest bit outside of a purely natural occurrence—I mean even crossing into feelings of intuition, unaccountable impressions and the like—I want you to let me know right away."

Florian simply nodded. He was not a man who easily tolerated being told how to do his job.

Charlot stood up, feeling slightly embarrassed. "I know you have told me that there is no pattern, that the causes of death have been all over the spectrum and entirely unsuspicious."

"Correct."

"Yet—" Charlot stopped herself. She had to wait for the autopsy results, then perhaps... "All right then. Carry on. As I said, don't hesitate to call me with anything. Any thought, *anything* that catches your notice, that might be relevant."

Florian nodded and got up to open the door. He was thinking about Selma, and the Chief's presence was irritating him.

"Women," he said to Matthias after she had gone. Florian rolled his eyes. "Nothing but trouble."

Molly's young friend Malcolm Barstow had not exactly set himself on a completely proper, law-abiding course since his father was sent to prison—he still dabbled in selling a few ounces of marijuana here and there, or contraband cigarettes, or a particularly noxious and herbaceous moonshine made by an ancient woman who lived up in the hills. But he was not a dedicated lawbreaker, only committing these small illegalities to get along while he tried to figure out what to do with his life. And still pals with Molly Sutton, as their paths had crossed several times and she had a soft spot for him, and he for her.

Malcolm was sort of the Madame Tessier of his generation—always knew the latest gossip, connected to all the various strata of Castillac society—and so the news of Delphine Bardot's passing came to him not long after she was discovered. He had seen Daisy the night before, had partied with her briefly in the decrepit house on the edge of the village, and guessed that she might not know what had happened. He set out to find her.

It was nearly nine o'clock and several guys were still sleeping in the decrepit house, their bodies huddled on the floor, using balled-up clothing as pillows. The house was unheated and Malcolm could see his breath as he searched the rooms. Daisy was not there.

Eventually he walked to the house on rue Malbec and knocked on the door. Daisy answered.

"Well, come in then, it's cold as ice," she said. She had not changed her clothes and seemed fully awake.

Malcolm looked at her carefully. She was not behaving like a person whose mother had just died—but he understood that he didn't know her well, so who really knows?

"How're you doing?" he said.

Daisy shrugged. "Castillac is a giant bore. As I'm sure I don't need to tell you."

Malcolm nodded. "You staying long?"

Daisy shrugged. "I want to get back to New York. I kept telling my mother, but she wouldn't listen. That's the thing, Malcolm—she never, ever listened."

Malcolm had not been an academic star, but he noted the verb tense. "You know?" he said softly.

"Some friend of hers came around and told me. Then that idiot gendarme came over."

Malcolm waited. He expected crying, or rage, or…something. But Daisy calmly walked to the refrigerator and looked in.

"No milk," she said simply. "I have to have milk in my coffee, so I'm going to the épicerie. Want anything?"

It didn't happen often but Malcom was speechless. He shook his head and watched as Daisy left the house, then followed her.

16

1994: New York City

PIERRE BARDOT CONSIDERED LIVING on Park or Fifth Avenue to be too flashy, so he installed his family in a brownstone on 73rd Street, just off Lexington Avenue. It had four stories, a basement, plus a decent-sized garden, and was only a few blocks from Central Park where his daughter Daisy wanted to go at any time, rain or shine.

His wife Delphine was used to small-town living, having grown up in Castillac, so she did not complain about not having a doorman or the other amenities often considered necessities by those in the Bardot's income bracket who lived in grand apartment buildings.

They were rich, even rich-rich, though of course in New York City, just emerging from the go-go 80s, money was apparently an endless flood and there were plenty of people richer than they.

Which kept Pierre Bardot up at night.

Which kept Pierre Bardot at the office so much of the time that his daughter, at age five, knew him as "Papa" but thought of him more or less as a stranger, who occasionally appeared and issued directives about this or that, which she and her mother would pretend to agree to and then ignore.

Overall, 211 East 73rd Street was not a happy home, despite all the money, the nanny, the designer clothes, the jewels, the credit cards, the car and driver, the five-star restaurants, and so on and so on.

One morning, the nanny called in sick. The back-up nanny didn't answer the phone. It was a Saturday and so there was no kindergarten; Pierre was at the office; hence Delphine was in charge of Daisy by herself.

"Shall we go to the Park?" Delphine asked, because she knew Daisy loved it, though the weather was turning cold and she herself did not want to go. What she wanted was to have a large glass of brandy and get back in bed.

"Yes!" shouted Daisy. "The Park, the Park, the Park!"

Delphine shushed her and told her daughter, for the millionth time, that good girls do not shriek. With some effort, she dressed the little girl in layers and gave her a wool cap with bunny ears. Delphine herself was still in pajamas. They were navy silk with white piping. She stood in her walk-in closet trying to decide what to put on and became so overwhelmed that she simply threw an oversized coat on over her pajamas, took Daisy by the hand, and headed out.

Even though her pajama bottoms were showing and she was towing a small child by the hand, Delphine was beautiful enough to capture the attention of the people she passed on the sidewalk. Men eyed her, tried to get her to look at them, one knocked into her on purpose—but Delphine was in her own world and paid them no notice.

"*Maman!*" shrieked Daisy. "Can we go to the monkey house and see the monkeys? Can we play hide and seek? Will you buy me some roller blades?"

"Shush," said Delphine. The attentions of her daughter were as intrusive as those of the men on the street. What she wanted was peace and quiet, the safety of no expectations, the freedom of not having to arrange a public face and make appropriate responses to people.

She was stuck on two questions, that took up almost every scrap of her attention: am I unhappy because of Pierre, or because of myself? And what, if anything, should I do about it?

When they got across Fifth Avenue, Daisy broke away from her mother and raced into a small grove of trees, kicking leaves and shrieking as loud as she could. Somewhere deep in the little girl's mind—more a feeling than a thought—was this: if I yell loud enough, will someone come take me away, and bring me to my real family?

17

"Oh, Molly—I don't believe we've been introduced? *Enchanté*, to be sure. I am André Baudelaire, notaire of Castillac, as I'm sure Ben has told you." He closed the door behind him, laughing a throaty sort of laugh that invited everyone else to laugh with him. "And this is my beloved, Blanchefleur Beauchêne."

Molly kissed cheeks with him and with Blanchefleur, and Ben took aperitif orders and went to make them.

"I'm so glad to meet both of you," said Molly. "Blanchefleur is such a lovely name, I've never heard it before."

"My mother was quite a romantic," said

Blanchefleur. "I believe I barely escaped being named Snow White."

They laughed and André looked at her with affection. "Blanchefleur is not a Castillacois, as you might have guessed," he said. "She's from Nice, that grand and most beautiful of cities. It's nothing short of a miracle that I have convinced her to stay in the village."

"Ah, Nice," said Molly. "It *is* the most beautiful city of all—Ben and I had our honeymoon there. But welcome to Castillac," she added, smiling at Blanchefleur, who shyly smiled back.

Ben listened to these pleasantries while he made the aperitifs—and a sparkling lemonade for Molly—noticing, not for the first time, that pregnancy seemed to have mellowed his wife. Her native impatience and restlessness had receded and in their place seemed to be a joyful acceptance of the present moment. No searching for excitement, for distraction, for...trouble.

And to be strictly honest, Ben wasn't entirely sure he favored this new placidity, though of course, novelty has something to say for it.

Molly asked how they met.

"Well, thanks for asking and it's an interesting story, though perhaps more interesting to Blanchefleur and myself than anyone else," said

André with a chuckle. "We met at the épicerie, of all the unromantic places. I was there for the usual reason a villager would be there—getting a bag of rice, I believe—and Blanchefleur was only passing through, driving to meet a girlfriend down in the Aude, near Carcassonne. She doesn't like driving on autoroutes and so her slow voyage took her through Castillac, and she stopped to buy a bottle of water."

"It's so lovely how so many wonderful things occur from random chance," said Molly, and Ben shot her a look. But she did not see the look and had taken Blanchefleur's hand. "And will you be staying...indefinitely?"

Blanchefleur blushed. André put his arm around her. "Only yesterday, she agreed to marry me," he said with a grin that nearly broke his face. "I am literally the happiest man alive."

"Congratulations!" said Ben, coming over with the drinks on a tray.

"Yes, hooray for you both," said Molly, grinning at them.

Still blushing, Blanchefleur spoke in a quiet voice. "I'm not sure...my family is...well...the situation is a bit unusual. You see, I am a relatively new widow. My trip to see a friend in the Aude was her attempt to cheer me up, because I have been so lost in grief for the last six months. So meeting

André—and falling in love with him—it was a surprise, to say the least."

André pulled her close and kissed the side of her head.

Ben took a sip of his pineau and then said, "Wonderful news." He asked a few questions about wedding plans, which the couple was pleased to talk about. "So," said Ben. "Shall we get the business out of the way so we can sit back and enjoy the rest of the evening? I shouldn't even bring it up at dinnertime, but the hours of these surveillance jobs—"

"Don't give it a thought," said André.

"We can cover it quickly, and then—Molly has made a *gratin Dauphinoise* that is so good it will make you weep."

"Oh, I look forward to that," said André. "Yes, sure, go ahead—you mentioned wanting a will?"

Ben described what he and Molly were looking for, and asked if André thought it appropriate. The discussion was short and they made plans to go to André's office whenever Ben's job ended to put everything in place.

"I would say there's certainly no big hurry. But lately, with the deaths in the village just piling up and piling up, maybe come on in and let's get this done," said André. "Not to sound excessively morbid."

"To be honest, I'm frightened," said Blanchefleur. "I think we all are, right?"

Molly shrugged. "I wouldn't say I'm frightened. Saddened, I guess. I'm sure before long, we'll find out an explanation. Or maybe not. I don't mean to sound unfeeling, but it does sort of amuse me how shocked people are when other people die. It's not like we haven't known this would happen since we were children. But we—and I include myself, of course—go through our lives as though that central fact about being a human on this earth is not really real. And then when someone dies, we are not only sad but surprised that the event could possibly have taken place, we feel as though all the rules of nature have suddenly been upended, when it is exactly the opposite."

"That's quite a speech, Molly," said André. Molly thought she heard an edge in his voice but wasn't sure. "I do see what you're saying, though. What are we up to now, five? Six? Don't you think—even accepting what you were just saying, and you do have a point—don't you think that's rather a lot in such a short time? Do you honestly believe these deaths are all natural?"

"Just tell the whole truth, chérie," said Blanchefleur. "Call them murder victims, because that's what they are." She looked at Molly to see if she agreed.

Molly shrugged. She smiled and drank her lemonade.

"For my part, I'd say I'm agnostic on the subject," said Ben. "Maybe there *is* a murderer on a mad spree. Or maybe…maybe these people are being poisoned somehow. Or—and I do lean this way, probably along with Molly—maybe the deaths are simply an unfortunate cluster on the graph of village deaths, nothing more than variance, and soon we will once again head into a long stretch where nobody dies at all and the villagers feel practically immortal."

"Can we talk of something else," said Blanchefleur. "It's just—it's too much—"

Molly was still holding the other woman's hand and she squeezed it again with a concerned look at her guest. Then, because she was pregnant after all, and it was close to eight o'clock, she yawned. An epic, impossible to disguise yawn, which set off a chain of yawning, first Blanchefleur and then Ben.

"I'm so sorry," Molly said, laughing, once the yawn was finally over. "I seem to get suddenly sleepy out of nowhere." She looked at André, who was drinking his drink with a blank expression, and worried for a moment that pregnancy had turned her formerly pretty good hosting skills to garbage.

SEVEN CORPSES ALL IN A ROW

THE NEXT MORNING, André lingered in the doorway, holding one of Blanchefleur's hands and stroking it.

"You're letting the cold air in," she said, giggling.

"I can't let go of you," he said. "I've always loved my job more than anything and now I find myself dreading leaving for work because I don't want to leave you."

"You are so silly," she said, but she beamed at him before looking away with shyness. Then she pulled him back inside and kissed him, luxuriantly, his hat falling to the floor as she wound her hands in his wavy hair.

"Ahh," he moaned, eyes closed. "You're not making this any easier."

"I think it's wonderful how you've offered to help these stricken families. Are you going to see any of them today?"

"Yes, I have knocked on a few doors so far, but only spoken to the son of one victim, who seemed very glad of my help. So that's promising."

Blanchefleur nodded, looking at the floor.

"Is something the matter, chérie?" he asked, gently lifting her chin so that she looked at him.

Blanchefleur's eyes welled up. "I—you have to get to work, I don't want—"

"I have all the time in the world for you," he said. "Tell me, what is wrong?"

She sighed and leaned against him, then pulled away. "The same old thing, really. Fear of...death!" she said, and then laughed darkly. "This fear can take many forms, as you well know. This morning, I've been worrying so much about Gabriel."

"But he's safe and sound at St. Anselm's, yes?"

"Well, yes, for the moment. But—what happens if I die suddenly like Louis did? He's already lost one parent, what if he loses the other? You and I know better than anyone how death can creep up and snatch you away with no warning."

André used his thumbs to wipe away her tears and then led her to the sofa and pulled her down next to him. He gathered her into a long hug, rubbing her back. "I know," he murmured. "My wife Marianne was so athletic, so fit, no one would ever have...."

Blanchefleur pulled back and looked at André, her eyes welling up again at the thought of how much pain he had endured. She kissed his forehead. "I know you know," she whispered. "And that is why I can't stop worrying about Gabriel. It's not really a financial thing, it's the idea of him being alone in the world, with no one to guide him, no one to care for him, and no one to celebrate when something good happens for him!"

"You are the dearest, most loving woman," said André, kissing her on the lips. "Would it ease your mind if I were his guardian? That way, if anything happened to you, I could take that role of guidance while he was still a child—and of course, I would hope to be friends so that the relationship would continue to grow after he was an adult."

Blanchefleur smiled, but it was not quite the wide smile of relief André was hoping for. "It's just..." She took in a great breath and heaved it out. "It's...that would be lovely of you, of course. And I thank you deeply for the offer. But the thing I'm *really* worried about..."

André waited patiently.

"...is that, well, the situation with his father, with Louis—I should have told you this before—is that...he was an alcoholic, in addition to being a workaholic. I know, I've probably painted such a rosy picture of our marriage, but the truth was less rosy by quite a bit."

André smoothed hair off her face and waited for her to finish.

"And so with Gabriel, what I worry most about, what keeps me up nights, is that as he gets older, as he goes through the inevitable teen period of rebellion and experimentation—what if he also develops some sort of addiction. Drugs, alcohol, whatever. You know there's a genetic component to these things. And what if he runs through his inheritance like it's water, and then has nothing and nobody. No life, no money, no love, only a mess of bad habits and an empty bank account."

"I'm so glad you shared that with me. It's lovely when a problem has such an easy solution! You can simply have something called a spendthrift trust drawn up, it's easy as pie. I've done it in my office, or you can have any lawyer do it for you. The money would be overseen by a third party, or only doled out on a schedule determined by you in advance. Gabriel would be protected no matter what foolishness he gets up to. And also, chérie—please don't assume the worst. He will be growing up and making his own way in the world, he won't automatically turn into his father. Or you either," he added with an affectionate smile.

"All right then," she said, laughing, "Now that you've solved all my problems, off with you! I'll make dinner tonight, something Parisian."

"I look forward to it more than words can say," he said, kissing her one more time before stepping back outside and closing the door.

Blanchefleur watched him walk down the short walk and then along the sidewalk. He looked back and winked at her, as she knew he would.

18

Constance arrived early on Changeover Day, shrieking as Bobo licked her face and immediately jumping into a long tale of woe about her boyfriend Thomas's latest transgression.

"Hold on just a minute," said Molly, sitting down to get a breath. "Rolanda is staying longer, so how about you trot over to the pigeonnier and ask if she'd like us to clean. The cottage is in pretty good shape but I'll give it a once-over—we've got a couple from Berlin coming today."

"Do you speak German? I don't," said Constance.

"*Auf weidersen* is all I got. But their English is good."

"I wasn't good at languages in school. Or math. Or—"

"Well, school is over so no worries," laughed Molly. She poured another cup of coffee. "So tell me about Thomas. What exactly has the poor lad done now?"

"I don't know why you call him poor lad. You can feel sorry for him after I break his head, which I'm about to!"

"Uh oh."

"Another ex-girlfriend has emerged."

"What do you mean, 'emerged'?"

"Risen from the swamp!" Constance said, flinging up her arms.

"Oh. The swamp of former girlfriends. I think I know that swamp."

"All women do!"

"Well, you can't convict Thomas for having former girlfriends. The past is the past. Unless… the past is suddenly present again?"

"You're muddling me up with all this talk of verb tense. I wasn't good at grammar either."

"I just mean—are you saying you just discovered she existed, or that Thomas is involved with her again?"

"You giving me coffee too or hogging it all for yourself?"

"Sorry. I'm distracted." Molly hopped up to get another cup.

"As well you might be, what with villagers dropping dead every five seconds."

"Let's get back to Thomas."

"Oh Molly, it's just…okay, I admit: *I'm* the problem. I'm so jealous. Like really really jealous even when I know in my head that Thomas isn't doing anything he shouldn't."

"So the ex is still ex."

Constance took the coffee from Molly and slumped her shoulders down. "Yes. As far as I know. I'm a lunatic."

"Indeed," said Molly. "We all are, sometimes. Shall we get the cleaning over with and make a nice lunch?"

"Sounds good. And you can tell me how you're going to catch the crazed serial killer that's mowing down villagers left and right."

🙢

MOLLY SIGHED and went to get the bucket and mop.

THE SATURDAY MARKET was showing its autumn version, with shoppers in down vests or sweaters, some wearing knitted caps; the fruit and vegetable selections were diminished from the height of summer, and several seasonal vendors had appeared with mushrooms and walnuts.

Daisy was up early; strictly speaking, she had not been to bed. She had a crumpled wad of euros in the pocket of her jeans, but it was not enough even for a few days' food. What had she and her mother been living on? Daisy didn't know. She didn't know if there was a bank account, or savings parked somewhere, or even some cash stashed away somewhere in their house.

Her ignorance was one more thing to be furious at her mother for.

Worry about money was a source of a nearly constant prickling in the back of her mind. Most of the time, she wasn't thinking about it directly. So far she had found that alcohol and pills only made the prickling erratic and sometimes muffled—it did not erase it. Not by any means. Sometimes it made it sharper, like a demon had sneaked up behind her and begun to stab her with a spike.

It was early enough that some of the vendors were still setting up. She heard a guffaw coming from behind a truck and glowered at the noise. She needed to eat, she could identify that much, but felt at a loss for what to do about it. Should she spend the little she had or would it be better to hold out as long as she could?

"Daisy?" A slim woman with erect posture had stopped in front of her.

Daisy looked at her and nodded before she could stop herself.

"Oh, chérie, I am so very sorry to hear the terrible news of your mother. I am Solange Forestier, we were good friends growing up."

Daisy froze. Images of her mother crowded into her mind—her mother as a teenager, hanging around with this woman, her mother sitting in the New York apartment holding a glass of brandy, her mother in the morgue.

She opened her mouth but had no words to say.

Solange took the liberty of putting an arm around her. "Why don't you come stay with me for a few days?" she said. "I know you don't know me, but this is a horrendous time and you—and I don't mean *you*, I mean *anybody*—shouldn't be alone. Do you have any friends in Castillac?"

Daisy pulled away. Solange thought her eyes looked like the eyes of a frightened animal.

"Well, bonjour, my beauties!" boomed a male voice, and Solange and Daisy turned towards it.

"Bonjour, André," said Solange.

"You're Delphine's daughter, am I right?" he

said to Daisy, who once again nodded before she could stop herself. More than anything, she wished these old people would leave her alone, but the manners her mother had instilled meant that she was unable to simply walk away.

"First of all, my deepest condolences. Losing your mother is one of life's most difficult passages, as I'm sure anyone who has been through it would tell you." His eyes welled up and he put a hand over his heart. "I was planning to come see you, Daisy," he said, taking her hands in his. "You know how it is—it's France after all!—so the paperwork you're going to face now, I'm sorry to say, is going to be mountainous. I would like, as a notaire, to offer my services and counsel for getting through it. Gratis, it goes without saying."

Does it? thought Solange, barely able to keep from rolling her eyes.

Daisy felt her throat close up and it was all she could do to stop herself from dropping to the ground and curling up in a ball.

Deceased. Her mother, deceased. Gone. *Dead*.

She put her hands over her ears and ran between two trucks and down an alleyway, vaguely heading in the direction of the dilapidated house, though not believing for a second that it would be any sort of haven.

19

The coroner's office was slow and had not yet released Delphine's body. Solange and the others were tired of waiting—was the French bureaucracy to burden not only life, but death?—and so they arranged for a memorial gathering to take place at a field just outside the village, beside a stream, telling her friends that the cemetery was too depressing. No one argued. They were used to Solange taking the lead, Solange doing what needed to be done.

And so they gathered on Saturday afternoon without a corpse to accompany them. Marielle walked the whole way with her arm around Daisy, who did not want to be there.

"Did you tell people?" she asked, judging the group to be too small.

"I can't do everything," said Solange.

Marielle started to say something but shook her head and pressed her lips together. The group trudged on, past Madame Renaud's house and then the Labiche farm, until they came to a wide field bordered by trees with most of the leaves fallen.

"Why again do we have to do this hike?" said Marielle, giving Daisy's shoulders a squeeze.

"You want a different funeral, you plan it," snapped Solange.

At last they stood next to the stream. Marielle told a funny story about the time Delphine dressed up in a fur coat she'd found at a *brocante* and fooled some newcomer to Castillac into believing she was a movie star. Manette cried softly into a handkerchief. Solange talked about how they used to tease Delphine for being the worst cook in all of France, and how she needed to marry a man rich enough that they could hire a cook.

"And then she went and did it," said Marielle, shaking her head with a feeling of admiration for the life Delphine had managed to build for herself. Even if it had all come crumbing down eventually.

Suddenly Daisy seemed to wake up and realize where she was. "You're all a bunch of phony fakers," she said, her voice gravelly. "Are you enjoying this big show of grief, is it fun for you?"

Marielle tried to get her arm around the girl again but Daisy shrugged her off. "You make me sick," she said, and took off across the field.

No one went after her. The friends looked at the urn and then at each other.

"Just doesn't seem fair," Marielle murmured. Manette held her hand. Solange searched for something to say and in that terribly sad moment found nothing.

Trudging along in the field, Daisy's legs felt heavy and insubstantial by turns, and she worried she wouldn't make it back to the village though it wasn't far. When she got to the road she stopped and put her hands on her knees, trying to get her breath.

Albertine, standing behind a boxwood bush, watched the girl intently. She blinked and blinked again, and did not otherwise move until Daisy was safely far down the road.

"It's too bad it took Delphine's taking a dirt nap to get us all together again," said Solange, as she poured herself three fingers of cognac and leaned back in her chair. The friends had come to her house for dinner, a continuation of the memorial proceedings. After the lamb stew was eaten, they stayed at the crumb-strewn table, candles flickering, the conversation finally turning serious.

"Dirt nap?" said Marielle. "I don't understand what you're talking about half the time, if I'm honest."

Manette just shrugged.

"People joke about death to make it less close," explained Solange.

"Always the professor," said Manette.

Solange grinned at her. "I've missed you people," she said.

"Well, we haven't gone anywhere," said Marielle.

Solange took a deep breath. "Look, I know I've been terrible about keeping up, I've been working on a book and barely left the house in months. I didn't even get to see Delphine again once she was back in the village. But you know...Delphine being back to Castillac gave me a jolt—it made me realize how I had let all the important connections in my life sort of...well, not go adrift. Let's say...slacken."

"Again, I never know what in hell you're talking about," said Marielle.

She put one arm around Solange and the other around Manette. "Let's just enjoy being together tonight. Delphine has just taught us that you never know what the next day will bring."

"Or if you'll even have a next day."

"Exactly," said Marielle. "I'm glad I saw her the night before she died—I was walking home from the épicerie and ran into her, she came over for a quick drink. Didn't stay long but now at least I have that memory."

"How did she seem?" asked Manette. "Did she look sick? The whole thing seems so sudden."

"Not sick at all," said Marielle.

The women exchanged glances. They drank more cognac.

Solange was tipsy and she kept her arm slung around Marielle's shoulders. "You know," she said, her voice conspiratorial, "I was thinking...I'm not saying Delphine was murdered. But if I had to choose one of us—I mean *us* from the old days, the four musketeers—I'd absolutely have picked Delphine as the one who would be murdered. If anyone was going to be."

Marielle gasped and then tried to cover it by sipping her drink.

"Doesn't seem like a compliment exactly," said Manette.

"I don't mean it as an insult. It's that—I don't think you can fight me on this—she was a magnet for bad men. For whatever reason. As we know better than most."

"It doesn't seem fair," murmured Marielle.

"You think the world is ever fair?" said Solange.

"Why in the world did she come back?" said Manette. "I mean, I was glad to see her and all. But..."

"Okay, just between us..." said Marielle in a low voice.

The other two waited. But they knew what she was going to say.

"Do you really think she might have been murdered?" Marielle whispered. As though the murderer was behind the door to the kitchen, listening in.

Manette shook her head as though refusing the possibility.

Solange shrugged. "Oh, you know me, I like to throw out what-ifs just for fun. I heard she died of a heart attack. Seems fitting, right? Like a cosmic joke."

The friends sat in silence, all thinking about the thing they didn't like thinking about.

"Maybe her marriage was happy?" said Manette finally.

"Well, and of course..." Solange started to say, but then changed her mind. "One thing about Delphine," said Solange, "she felt things intensely. It's not everyone who moves to a new continent to get over a breakup."

The other women nodded again. "That was not exactly your garden-variety breakup," Marielle said.

"All those years ago, and the fury about what he did is still so fresh."

"I know," said Marielle. "And doesn't it seem crazy, looking back, that we never told anyone? Never asked for help?"

Solange nodded. "I know. But we were young. And scared. After what he did to Delphine, and then threatening you…"

Marielle shuddered.

"And then who did she get with the minute she came back? That utterly useless Milo Clavel."

"Useless is the least of it," said Solange, drumming her fingers on the table.

Quietly they thought more about their old friend while staring at a guttering candle, each of them feeling the fear that came with thinking about the possibility of murder, especially after all the other recent deaths, coming one right after another.

They were in silent agreement that speaking about these things would only make the fear worse.

But not speaking about them made them feel lonely…and even more scared.

20

Sunday evening was usually the busiest night of the week at Chez Papa. After a day of lounging around at home and eating a big meal with family, many villagers wanted a drink and a change of pace, as well as a new cast of characters, even if it was the same cast of characters they saw nearly every Sunday night at Chez Papa.

That Sunday, Milo Clavell was taking center stage, crying about Delphine as he drank glass after glass of a cheap local red another man kept buying for him. A few others—the sort of people drawn to car wrecks—patted Milo on the shoulder or murmured words of comfort, which only seemed to increase his distress. After a long gulp of wine, Milo took off his ratty scarf and combed his fingers through the short fringe, then wound it around his neck, tight as a bandage.

"She was my heart and soul," he murmured, and when no one responded, he said it more loudly.

Lapin and Anne-Marie were at the bar, talking to Frances. "I wish that guy would crawl back into his hole," said Lapin.

"What in the world did Delphine see in him?" asked Anne-Marie.

"Delphine had the worst taste in men, bar none," said Lapin. "Of course, I never met her husband. I don't think they ever came to Castillac after they were married—but I can tell you with certainty that he was no good, because that was apparently a requirement for her."

"Sad," said Frances. "I mean, I took a few wrong turns in my past—maybe we all have?—but I didn't make it a habit."

"Glad to hear it," said Nico, giving her a side-eye.

Frances squeezed Luka's feet and grinned at him. "But so why is everyone talking nonstop about Delphine, anyway? There's this whole heap of other dead people we could be gossiping about, but no one seems very interested. What's that about?"

"Molly should be asking questions," murmured

Lapin. Anne-Marie put her arm around him, and Nico cocked his head, then nodded.

"It's not like she's head of the gendarmerie," said Frances. "She's just a private citizen like the rest of us."

Lapin gave her a withering look.

"Well, maybe the reason she's not asking questions is that there is no murderer! Have you considered that?" said Frances, loud enough that people down the bar leaned forward to see what was going on. "I mean, we *know* her," said Frances. "It's not like Molly is going to allow the village to be ravaged by some crazed serial killer while she sits back looking at the clouds go by!"

"Your loyalty is notable," said Lapin. "But you must realize, given the small being which has been attached to you for the last few months, that a pregnant Molly may not be the Molly we know."

"What is *that* supposed to mean?" said Frances, about to hand off Luka to Nico so she could take a fighting stance, dukes up.

Lapin shrugged the most Gallic of shrugs.

"She is rather changed, it seems to me," said Anne-Marie in a quiet voice.

"Well then, come on, why are we sitting around going 'Boo-hoo-hoo Molly isn't saving us'? We've seen how she works. She settles on something and then digs at it and digs at it. Surely the lot of us can do the same? Aren't five of us equal to one Molly?"

No one appeared to think so. They fidgeted and looked down at their shoes like a pack of *primaire* students.

"The first death—who knew this Olivia Miller person, for starters? She lived over on, uh, rue whatchamacallit, down the street from Madame Tessier. Had that enormous vegetable garden, come on, you must know it. And a gazillion dogs, all shapes and sizes. You'd come down the street and the howling would start up."

"Maybe one of her neighbors did her in because the howling had driven them crazy."

"Does anyone know what her cause of death was?"

Long silence.

"You people are useless," said Frances, giving up.

"Exactly!" said Lapin, perking back up. "We absolutely *are*, which is why we have to figure out how to convince Molly to get to work!"

"It's Sunday night," said Nico. A chill fell over the group. They all understood what he meant. The most commonplace of statements now had a different meaning.

"This is when it happens," said Anne-Marie, barely louder than a whisper.

A crash.

"Stop being an idiot, Milo!" shouted a man in grimy clothes and an incongruously neat moustache.

Milo sank down into a chair and put his face in his hands.

"And quit play-acting!" said the man with the moustache. "We've had it with you! You want theatrics, go join a theater club somewhere. Preferably somewhere far, far away."

"Hear hear," someone said.

Milo drew himself up and lifted his nose in the air. "Clearly you have no experience with grief," he said. He stepped over to the chair he had thrown moments earlier, and set it back upright. "And I congratulate you on that, because grief is so powerful, so unbearable, I fear it may be my undoing!"

"Oh for heaven's sake," said Anne-Marie. "Could he be more ridiculous?"

"What *I* was thinking is," said Frances, leaning on the bar and lowering her voice, "what better disguise for a serial killer than being ridiculous?"

Lapin and Nico looked at her.

"That's not half bad," said Lapin. "Come on now, keep going…"

"Well, it's obvious, right?" said Frances. "Isn't being the most grief-stricken of all an age-old way for a killer to hide? Milo acts like he and Delphine had been together for thirty years of bliss instead of two weeks of arguments. I don't buy his act for one tiny second."

Nico, Lapin, and Anne-Marie all nodded, eyes widened.

"Maybe we should tail him," said Lapin, trying to whisper and failing. "Sunday night is the Death Night, right? So we shouldn't let him leave here and go off to do...whatever he's got in mind," he added with a slight shiver.

"It's what Molly would do," said Frances.

They all nodded again. But not one of them had the slightest intention of following Milo Clavel anywhere.

MOLLY AND BEN were regulars at Chez Papa on Sunday nights, but on that particular Sunday, Molly had been feeling twinges in her belly that were a little unsettling, and she didn't feel like going out. So instead they lit a fire in the woodstove and settled on the sofa with a blanket, Bobo at their feet, and cups of cocoa with whipped cream.

"It's Sunday," said Ben quietly.

Molly nodded, knowing what he meant.

"So what's your guess?"

Molly considered. She closed her eyes and

waited a moment, checking to see whether a thought, a feeling, a sensation, anything at all—might lead her thoughts one way or another. She felt another twinge in her abdomen, put her hand on it, and sighed.

"Well, I don't know, obviously. What about you?"

"Do you think it meaningful that there has never been more than one death in a day?"

"Maybe."

"It does seem like if it is a serial killer, killing one at a time would clearly be more manageable. If you were at all interested in not getting caught."

Molly said nothing.

"As to my guess," said Ben, "I don't have one. I think it's entirely likely that Florian is correct and there is nothing suspicious going on. And of course we *want* to believe that is true. And yet..."

"...and yet..."

"And what about the Sunday angle," said Ben. "What is that about?"

"I don't know," said Molly. She pulled the blanket up to her chin and snuggled closer. She closed her eyes again.

"Do you want to go to bed?" Ben asked, feeling her relax against him.

She shook her head but did not speak.

"Earlier, when I was fixing that broken window,

I was grouping the victims in circles," said Ben. "By age, sex, nationality."

"I've done similar. Got nowhere."

Ben smiled because he knew that Molly, no matter what she said or how unenthusiastic she seemed, had been turning the situation over in her mind. She was keeping close track of the details, as she always did.

"Me neither. Anyway, I thought maybe we could assume for a moment that the older group had simply died from natural causes because they were all old enough for that to be—let's say—not unusual. Not immediately suspicious. Especially with their causes of death all being different. But—of course—that does not preclude some of the deaths being murders even if all of them are not.

"It has been hard for me since the beginning to believe that anyone would kill Lucien Pugh, for example. He was not the kind of guy you can imagine stirring that much bad feeling."

"But you know murder isn't always about that. His killer could be someone who enjoyed that very quality about him—who felt that Lucien's mildness made him even more appealing as a target. Not every murder is about a beef or money or revenge. If these *are* murders—and as I've continually been saying, I don't think they are—why would a killer want to do most of the killing on Sundays? Even if we caught this purported murderer, isn't it possible we might never know the answer to that?"

"In other words, I should stop trying to make sense out of something that might be senseless. You know I do know that. But I find my mind keeps trying anyway."

Molly tightened her arms around him. "Let's not talk about it anymore," she said softly. "It's Sunday. So what happens tonight will happen, and then we'll see."

This sort of resignation in the face of deaths in the village was not, obviously, usual for Molly; it gave Ben a quick flash of anxiety. He hugged her back, kissed the top of her head, and the two of them stayed on the sofa watching the light flicker in the woodstove until it was very late.

21

Chief Charlot got the call early Monday morning, not long after dawn.

She had been up for hours, unable to sleep because no amount of reassurance from Florian had been able to settle her mind about the six deaths of villagers.

And now it was seven.

Her uniform was pressed and ready and as she got dressed it felt as though her limbs had weights on them. The feeling of dread that had been kindling in her lower belly was now insistent and difficult to ignore.

Charlot drove to the house of the deceased. Florian's white van was already parked outside.

"So many months of calm…" she said, by way of greeting.

"…and now *le déluge*," answered Florian.

She looked at the body, which Florian and Matthias had already gotten onto the stretcher.

"He looks in very good shape," said Charlot.

"Apart from being dead, yes," said Florian.

Matthias bit the side of his cheek, feeling anxious. He much preferred the office part of his job and had been trying to convince his boss to hire someone else to accompany him when he picked up bodies—so far, unsuccessfully.

"You know him?" asked Florian.

Charlot shook her head.

"Early sixties, farm worker. His neighbor called my office to report the death."

"What was his neighbor doing here?"

"She said that they took walks together on Sunday mornings at dawn, had done so for years. When she knocked on his door, he—obviously—did not answer."

"Sorry, am I missing something? The neighbor says they walked on Sunday mornings, so why did she call you early on Monday morning?"

"She did not say and I did not ask. That's your department."

"Name of the neighbor?"

"Marielle Salomon."

"Ah, I know her. She works at the épicerie on the weekends."

"Just so."

"How did she get in?"

"Door was open."

"So she said."

"So she said."

"Cause of death?"

"Don't pin me down before the autopsy. But my guess—and it's a fairly firm one, for what that's worth—we're talking heart attack."

All three of them stood with their eyes on the corpse. No one said any prayers because not one of them was religious, but they did take a pause and feel sorry for him. After some long moments, Florian drew a sheet up over the body and instructed Matthias about maneuvering the stretcher through the narrow doorway of the house.

Charlot thanked Florian and got into her car and sat.

She put her hands on the steering wheel and squeezed it as hard as she could.

She was a well-trained, disciplined, accomplished officer who had finished near the top of her class—Chantal Charlot was not one for giving in to emotion. Yet as she sat in her car in the early morning light, shivering from the damp, she sensed that the spate of deaths in the village were not, as Florian insisted, all due to natural causes. She felt it to be so and she trusted that feeling. She understood that something or someone was killing them, and of course it was her job to figure out how and why and put a stop to it.

Yet still, some part of her kept arguing back, saying that the most basic understanding of statistics would say this number of deaths was simply the way numbers worked, that it was contrary to the laws of mathematics to expect that people would die on some regular schedule. There were no deaths, and then a lot. Nothing to be made out of that, nothing unusual, all she had to do was put one foot in front of the other and over time, the numbers would adjust. Molly Sutton had made this point to her before, and Charlot had to understand the truth of it, to trust it and proceed accordingly—no, the problem was not understanding but acceptance.

In her heart, she believed otherwise. But for some reason, the reassurance that routine police work usually offered—that if you go through the steps, methodically and without emotion, you will get closer and closer to the truth—felt thin and not reliable.

She knew there was murder going on. She simply had no ideas on where to begin.

SEVEN CORPSES ALL IN A ROW

LAPIN WAS VERY fond of mornings, especially Monday mornings. After a leisurely coffee with Anne-Marie, he drove into the village and opened his shop, and the regularity of these two consecutive actions, six days a week, always the same, were calming and reassuring to him. One of the things he loved about Castillac was its predictability: he knew as he put the shop key into the lock that just then his friend Edmond Nugent was taking fresh baguettes out of the oven over at Patisserie Bujold, and likely plotting some new recipe that would expand Lapin's girth even further.

He knew that Madame Tessier would soon be seated in her chair in the small yard in front of her house, soaking up every wisp of gossip that passed her way.

He knew that the gendarmes were at the gendarmerie, the children were at school, the priest was at the church, and everyone and everything was just where it should be.

He knew that Delphus McDougal would come in to paw through the bowls of costume jewelry and ask for what seemed the millionth time to look at the de la Chabelle dinner service.

He knew that after sweeping up and doing a bit

of dusting, he would stroll over to a hole-in-the-wall café and have another cup of coffee.

Six days a week, always the same, and Mondays were appreciated as the day the routine started up again.

And also, Lapin knew that if anyone in Castillac died in a suspicious way—even if the death did not seem fishy at all to most people—his friend Molly Sutton would be on top of the situation, no matter how much interference and pushback she got from the other villagers, the gendarmerie, or the circumstances themselves. Which was a sort of security Lapin was grateful for, and had come to depend on.

He was in the back, cleaning out the many drawers in an unusual little desk he had recently acquired, when the bell on the door tinkled, announcing a customer. Lapin was momentarily disappointed to see that it was André, since he had never bought a single item in the shop and over their long acquaintance had never shown the slightest interest in antiques.

"Bonjour, André," said Lapin, wiping his hands on his pants.

"You're up early."

"I am always in the shop at this hour. It is *you* who is up early," said Lapin with a laugh.

"You heard?"

Lapin's stomach dropped. He shrugged. For a moment he wished that whatever it was, André would decide not to tell him, but his natural desire to know all the business of the village won out. "What," he said, squeezing his eyes shut.

"Number seven," said André, shaking his head.

"What a ray of sunshine you are," said Lapin.

"Worked for the big farm over at Salliac. Heart attack supposedly. But the man was fit—physical work outdoors, you understand, day in and day out, for a lifetime. Only in his sixties. Not exactly a heart attack prospect."

Lapin glanced down at his own belly and took a deep breath. "I don't know what you're implying."

"Settle down, Lapin!" André laughed. "I'm not insulting you. I came over to ask you something. I've been feeling…well, I don't like even saying the word, but…helpless, really. I had a couple of ideas, if I could bounce them off you?"

"Sure," said Lapin, though he wasn't remotely interested.

"It's just—all the deaths that has me on edge. I was wondering if we could come up with a way for the village to show support. Maybe organize a dinner, like we have on fête day?"

Lapin scowled and shrugged. "I don't see what good that would do. What would help is getting some reassurance that the deaths are legit, natural deaths and not something…else."

"You don't trust Florian?"

Lapin shrugged again. They stood for a moment in silence. Lapin felt a tightness in his chest. *Seven?* He saw the number dancing in the air, and felt a flash of panic that he was seeing things that weren't there. André was gazing through the shop window at the street, lost in thought. Finally Lapin shrugged again. "Seven. Seven people. In how many weeks? How are we supposed to handle that?"

André stroked his chin. "I don't know what to think," he said in a low voice. "It certainly doesn't feel natural, does it?"

"It does not," said Lapin, his voice cracking like he was fourteen.

22

Molly was restless, but after the seventh death did not want to go into the village and subject herself to more importuning. So she called Lela Vedal to ask if it was a good time for her to come out and see Tempête work the goats. It was, and she threw on a scarf—never able to get it quite as chic as the Frenchwomen—and took the scooter out to the farm.

Tempête trotted over when Molly arrived and gave her a cursory sniff.

"Bonjour, Molly!" said Lela, coming over with a bucket in each hand. "Honestly, she's much more interested in goats than people. Wait 'til you see her at work!"

Lela set the buckets next to the barn, and they

walked down a path, through a meadow, Tempête in the lead.

"It's so cool to be able to see the actual goats whose milk makes my favorite cheese," said Molly.

"See how this pasture is recovering so nicely, now that it's not being grazed," said Lela. "It's driven me crazy for years, having all this land right next door but my neighbor refused to sell it to me. Absolutely refused even though it was lying fallow. He was actually paying someone to mow it a couple of times a year so it wouldn't get overgrown."

"And finally relented? Do you know why?"

"Yes, at last! Every year I would make him an offer, maybe he just got sick of me."

They got to the top of a rise and Molly could see the herd of goats in the distance. The dog shot ahead, her body low to the ground, and she moved with incredible speed to the left of the herd, making a wide circle. The goats tossed their heads and some of them bucked. But they did, however grudgingly, move the way Tempête wanted them to.

"Amazing," said Molly. "Aren't dogs just the best?"

"Well, I have a soft spot for goats," said Lela. "But dogs too. She gets so much joy from having a job."

SEVEN CORPSES ALL IN A ROW

They watched for some time in silence. Lela was not giving Tempête any instruction and so the dog ran loops around the goats, not forcing them into a tight group, and the goats spread out. Some went along the fence and did some voracious grazing, even sticking their heads into the next pasture though they had plenty to graze where they were.

Molly was looking at the ground by her feet. "So many different kinds of plants," she said. "Do you seed the pastures or is all this just what nature provides?"

"Seed? Oh no. Thankfully, as that would add quite a cost to the operation. It's funny though—goats prefer to browse rather than graze. That means they like to reach up for their food. See those poor little saplings over there—they've stripped the leaves right off them. But of course they graze as well—they'll just eat whatever is growing in the fields. That's one great thing about raising goats—they love weeds and will eat just about anything!"

Molly closed her eyes and felt grateful for the feeling of the warm sun on her skin, the bleating of the goats, and, of course, the baby. And then the almost ever-present hunger returned and she said her goodbyes to Lela and went in search of lunch.

23

The mood in the village had only deteriorated further by Wednesday, as news of the latest death reached every corner of Castillac, with no observable action or even so much as a comment by the gendarmerie.

Chantal and Paul-Henri were at their desks. The tension on the street was such that walking his usual beat was uncomfortable for Paul-Henri, so he rummaged up some paperwork to do instead. And Chief Charlot sat with her computer off, not pretending to do anything, her fingers sometimes drumming the top of her desk or tapping her thumb in quick succession.

"I don't know how," she said finally, "but Florian is wrong."

Paul-Henri looked up. "Are you sure?"

"Of course I'm not sure," she snapped. "But his conclusions make no sense. Don't talk to me about statistics, I've been around that block a hundred times already. And forget the other deaths, let's just talk, right now, about Monsieur Belmont. A strong, fit man—not under any stress, his life as regular as clockwork—suddenly dies in his sleep? It's not…it's not right. Don't you—can't you sense the *wrongness* of that? I'm not talking only about his health. I'm…I'm talking about…one's general expectations, one's feeling of how the world works, one's…overall sense of things," she whispered, knowing that she had traveled so far from the prescribed methods and techniques of the gendarmerie that Paul-Henri would be shocked.

And indeed, he looked stupefied. His hands dropped to his sides and his face slackened. "My sense?" he said, in a small voice.

"Seven deaths!" Charlot shouted, jumping up from her desk. "You're going to sit there and tell me you believe they died of this or that, then another, and another, and another? Still this or that? Heart, kidney, pick your organ! While we sit here accomplishing nothing! Laughingstocks of the village, of the *département*, of all of France!"

Paul-Henri kept very still. He blinked. Then he took a deep breath and said, "Since you asked my opinion, I will say that I believe Florian is correct, and while unfortunate, the seven deaths do not proceed from ill intent. We have worked with him all these years, and when has he ever been wrong? Well, apart from that one…never mind. Nonetheless, now you are saying he is suddenly wrong seven times in a row? Excuse me, Chief, but that does not compute. I don't believe Florian is having some kind of crisis that would make his work unreliable. I know he's been suffering from heartbreak—everybody knows, as he moans about it nonstop—but I don't think that would make the conclusions of the office of the coroner, which he takes very seriously, suddenly be the stuff of hallucination."

"It would hardly be the first time that someone's private life interfered with his job. He is distracted, at the very least. And I wonder if he is not simply signing off on these causes of death in the most slapdash fashion, just to clear his desk so he can bang on about that British woman."

Paul-Henri didn't know what else to say.

"Then give me an alternative explanation," said Charlot. "Please. Go ahead."

"It's just bad luck," said Paul-Henri.

Charlot laughed at that, a dark laugh that gave Paul-Henri a chill. She did not reply but shook her head, and stood up. She stood breathing hard for a moment and Paul-Henri was reminded of a racehorse after a sprint, her nostrils wide and huffing.

"I'm going out. What I want you to do is put away that paperwork and get to work on death number seven, Belmont. Talk to his friends, talk to his family. See if there is any bad blood in any direction, any arguments, any long-standing grievances, from any side. If there is the slightest possibility that Monsieur Belmont was murdered, I want you to find that out. Standard police work will get you there. Understand?"

"Yes, Chief," said Paul-Henri, jumping to his feet. He wanted to check his uniform in the mirror to make sure all the buttons were present and shining, but he didn't dare.

"When you're done with that, you can give me a verbal report on Belmont. And then begin at the beginning with death number one followed by number two. Talk to the neighbors, find out what they did in the days before they died—did they take money out of the bank? Did they argue with anyone? What time did they generally get up and go to bed? What were their habits, as far as the neighbors could tell?"

"That is a lot," said Paul-Henri, without meaning to.

"Yes indeed," said the Chief. "It *is* a lot. A lot of death, piled up at our doorstep. We've been taking

Florian's pronouncements as absolute truth, when —not to cast aspersions on him—*anyone* can be wrong. We should have started investigating with the first death, and now we are dreadfully behind. Something is killing our constituents. And we had better get to the bottom of who or what if we want to save some lives. Not to mention hold on to our jobs."

Paul-Henri looked stricken and moved quickly to get his coat. They left the gendarmerie together, faces grim.

24

"So...we're up to seven," said Madame Tessier, as Molly settled into the chair next to her, after kissing cheeks.

"Yes we are," said Molly.

Madame Tessier was a merry sort who usually had a twinkle in her eye and a smile on her face, but not that day. "I was childhood friends with Belmont," she said. She pressed her lips together before continuing; Molly thought she saw tears gathering and then Madame Tessier squeezed them back. "Back a million years ago, he and I loved to play hide and seek—I mean we were, as eight-year-olds, completely obsessed with it! And you know how those early bonds can last. We hardly saw each other once we left school, but every time I did see him, I felt eight years old again and we both would have a delicious memory of the thrill we used to feel as children, tearing around outside having so much fun, so free and excited to be alive."

Molly reached over and put her hand on Madame Tessier's. "There is something so sorrowful yet lovely in what you say," said Molly, who had at least one old friend like that: the complicated Frances.

"It feels melancholy, right now. Of course I will miss his presence in the village, and he was taken before his time, to be sure. But also—I have such joyful memories of my time with him, and I am grateful for that." Madame Tessier smoothed her dress over her knees and looked at Molly. "First, let me inquire about the baby? How is everything? How are you feeling?"

Molly grinned and patted her bump. "All is well. I don't feel like throwing up all the time anymore, so this is major progress."

"I should say so." Madame Tessier smiled, but the smile faded immediately. "Well, then?" she said.

Molly sighed. She patted her belly again. "Well what?"

"What's going on, obviously, with the seven deaths. I know you have thoughts."

Molly shrugged.

"Now, don't shrug at me, for heaven's sake," said Madame Tessier. "It can't be missing your notice that many villagers think we're being decimated by a serial killer. Nor can you be missing that those same people wish you would get moving and solve the case! As you do."

"I seem to have given the impression I could fix all the problems, when I have no such powers."

"Oh now," said Madame Tessier, and her laugh was infectious. "No one's putting *all* the problems at your feet. It's only specific problems we want you to work on," she said. "The ones involving murder."

They sat in silence for a moment.

"As I don't have to tell you," Madame Tessier murmured.

Molly's eyes were on the linden tree across the street. She watched a leaf fall into the gutter, and did not answer.

"I'm sorry I never met Ginette Duchamps," Molly said finally.

"Well, you can put that regret to one side—you were never going to meet her."

Molly's eyebrows went up.

"Nothing personal," said Madame Tessier. "Ginette was a recluse. Never left the house. Or the *manoir*, I should say."

"Did you know her before she stopped going out?"

"Oh, back in the day, I saw her in the village, here and there. But we were not friends, or even acquaintances. She was…snooty."

"Aristocratic?"

"Not actually, I don't believe. Well, I suppose Duchamps is a decent name, as far as it goes, but it was her husband's name. There was certainly no title, nothing like that, I think her late husband made his money selling lightbulbs. But she used to swan around the village as though everyone should be taking a knee when she went by."

"Mm," said Molly.

Madame Tessier waited, expecting Molly to ask more questions, but Molly seemed more interested in a cat that was winding its way underneath a car and then around a bicycle leaning up against a railing, and said nothing at all.

It was nearing eleven at night when Albertine Dupont, on her usual walk, passed by the house of Lucien Pugh. The moon was hidden behind clouds and the streetlight was out, so she could barely see where she was going.

She stopped and stared at Lucien's house. Then she rolled her shoulders back several times, spat on Lucien's gate, and moved off down the street.

25

Daisy woke near dinnertime, with the sun already gone, in the dilapidated house on the edge of the village, in between several bodies that were dreaming, not dead. Daisy knew they were alive but nevertheless their stillness made her shiver.

What have I done, she murmured to herself, over and over, rubbing her hands briskly over her arms and then lying down again, hoping for the unconsciousness of sleep but not hopeful she would get it.

She lay with her eyes squeezed shut, listening. A car drove past. She heard no birds, no wind, nothing but the occasional stirring from someone in the next room who was, from the sound of it, opening packages. Bags of chips, or something like that.

The crinkling of the bags was like fingernails on a blackboard to Daisy, and she squeezed her eyes tighter though the effort of doing so took her yet farther from sleep.

"Come on, now," said a voice near her ear. Her eyes flew open and she saw Malcolm.

She made some sort of sound, between a grunt and a moan.

"That's lovely," he said. "Now come on, sit up and pull yourself together. I'm taking you out of here to get something to eat."

Eat? She wanted to be asleep, not talking to this boy or any boy, but the rest of her—her stomach, of course, especially—said hold on a minute, there's food? And so she gave in and sat up.

Malcolm led her outside and then stepped back to take a look at her. "You look like something the cat dragged in," he said.

"Thanks," said Daisy.

"I'd take you to mine to clean you up but…it's complicated. Let's go to your place."

"No."

"You got another idea? It's not like I've got super high standards," he said, laughing. "But seriously, you look…you look like you've been rolling around in an alley for a week, and bugs might be crawling out of your hair. We can't go anywhere in public until you clean up a little. Or—do you *want* to be attracting attention?"

Daisy shook her head and they started to walk to her house.

Neither spoke. She had nothing she wanted to say to anyone. Malcolm was smart enough to keep his mouth shut.

When they got a block away from the house, Daisy slowed down, then stopped. Malcolm observed her.

"I...I don't want to go in there," she whispered. Her voice was rough, as though she had something stuck in her throat.

"I get it," he said. "But you can't keep avoiding it. Your stuff is inside, your clothes and everything. Your mother is...she's not there now. There's nothing to be afraid of."

Daisy stood staring down at the sidewalk. She shook her head, kept shaking it.

"You're not a ghost, no matter how much you wish you were." He took her arm and squeezed it gently. "Come on back to the actual world," he said.

She put her hands on her hips and Malcolm thought she was going to refuse. But then her hands dropped and she swayed for a moment, then fell to the street in one motion, like her bones had suddenly turned to mush and there was nothing left to hold her upright.

⁂

EARLY FRIDAY MORNING, Ben left early for his surveillance job and Molly, without even realizing what she was doing, found herself parking the scooter outside Patisserie Bujold and entering to the tinkle of a bell, Edmond's first customer of the day.

"What a delight you are to the eyes," said Edmond, beaming at her. "You usually come on Saturdays. To what do I owe this splendid disruption of habit?"

"I need an almond croissant, stat," she said. "And bonjour, by the way, lest you think I have lost my manners."

"I give you a pass for the duration of your pregnancy."

"Really? Are pregnant women known for being ill-mannered?"

"Not at all, not at all," he said soothingly. "It is more—in my experience only, you understand, which you must take with a healthy pinch of salt—that women who are with child can be quite vocal about what they need at any particular moment.

Which is not unmannerly in the least, but sometimes they might feel that it is."

"Sometimes you talk nonsense," said Molly. "Now, um, where is that croissant? Because when I said 'stat' I wasn't kidding around."

"It's quite early," said Edmond. "They are still in the oven. You have only a moment to wait."

Molly lifted her nose in the air and inhaled. Patisserie Bujold had the most intoxicating smell, of vanilla and sugar and yeast and coffee. And in that moment, Molly wanted all those things desperately. In great quantities, and as soon as possible.

"Have a seat and I will serve you," said Edmond, bustling behind the counter. He went into the back where the ovens were and plucked out a croissant though they still had half a minute to go. The espresso machine hissed and he folded a cloth napkin into a swan and set it on a tray.

"Here you are, chérie," he said, putting the tray down with a flourish.

Before he could say what was on his mind, Molly had jammed nearly the entire croissant in her mouth and was moaning slightly, eyes closed.

"You just cannot understand," she said, "how much I want to eat. I mean to tell you—it is *nothing* like simply being hungry. I am consumed by a sort of ravenous appetite that I—I can't even describe it. It overtakes *everything*."

"Would you like another?" said Edmond, a bit appalled by her display.

"Make it two," said Molly.

Edmond scurried back to the oven and took out the tray of croissants. He checked the progress of the sourdough and got out some trays for his next task, then took the warm croissants to Molly.

"It's just…*ohh*," she said, eyes closed. "It's not exactly news that I love an almond croissant. But these almond croissants? Best things I have ever eaten in my life. No exaggeration." She pulled one into two pieces, admiring the stretchy layers, and a chunk of marzipan fell to the saucer next to a slice of almond.

"I'm not sure I have ever seen the act of eating be so…so…passionate," he said, lowering his eyes.

The friends sat in silence as Molly drank her espresso and finished the third croissant.

Then she burped.

"Excuse me," she said, giggling, and giggling harder seeing Edmond's shocked expression.

"My gracious," he said. He got up and walked nervously to the door and looked out. "All right, listen Molly, enough fun and games."

Molly waited, knowing exactly where he was headed.

SEVEN CORPSES ALL IN A ROW

"Seven villagers are dead! *Seven!* And I would like to know—no excuses, now—what you plan to do about it."

"Do? I don't know what magic you people think I have. This situation is not…it's not about me," she said, slapping a hand on the little table for emphasis and making the saucer clatter.

"There's no need for violence," said Edmond, lifting his nose in the air. "I merely asked when you thought you might continue the job you have been doing so ably, so very ably, ever since you moved to Castillac."

"I don't know *anything*, Edmond. I don't know if any of the seven deaths are natural, or not. Florian, I will remind you, says they not suspicious at all. So why everyone is jumping on me to prove him wrong, I do not know. I understand that death makes people jittery, of course I get that. And sure, all right, we find somebody dead from a gunshot wound, or someone's head has been bashed in—these are fairly clear murders and yes, thank you, I have had some success with that sort of thing.

"But what's happening now is *not* that sort of thing and I cannot explain it. I cannot proceed in my usual fashion because this situation is…something else. I do not know what that is. If I could stop people from dying, believe me I would! But I do not have that sort of power. Do you understand?"

Again she brought her palm to the top of the little table and smacked it.

"Well, what *I* say is that it *is* that sort of thing and the only difference is one of scale, which means it's even more imperative that you get a move on," said Edmond. "And now, if you'll excuse me, I have pastries to make and bread to bake. Good day to you."

Molly paid and left. She walked to her scooter, her thoughts not clarified by the espresso or her friend's chilly goodbye.

She didn't actually disagree with Edmond. She did not believe Castillac was being ravaged by a serial killer, though of course, she reminded herself, she didn't know one way or the other. But for whatever reason, seven felt way more than six, it felt... *off*. It was undeniably frightening.

However. She did not see a way forward. Seven deaths, with different causes, how does one even begin? Molly fervently wanted to do nothing but enjoy the brisk autumn weather, learn how to knit, daydream about her baby, and eat enormous and fabulous meals with Ben, preferably multiple times a day.

Was that so much to ask? If something was

afoot—and she wasn't admitting, even to herself, that it was—why couldn't someone else step up, just this once? What were Chantal and Paul-Henri doing, anyway?

※

THEY WERE—SINCE dawn—inside the gendarmerie, going over every collected fact and trying to see where they led. Paul-Henri kept yawning, exhausted after the long days he'd been putting in. The Chief's face was stony.

"I did a pretty thorough job on Belmont," said Paul-Henri. "But I turned up exactly nothing. He did not lead a complicated life. He was not married. He worked at the same farm for his entire adulthood, and he was friendly with his neighbors, who didn't have a bad word to say about him. Belmont was a man of strict routines: he took a long walk with his neighbor, Marielle Salomon, every Sunday morning, right at dawn. Every week, he came early to the market on Saturdays and got his meat from Raoul, vegetables from Manette, wine from the vineyard in Sallière. Once a month or thereabouts he drove to one of the big shops outside of Bergerac to get various household goods. As far as I can tell, he spent upwards of forty years eating the same things and doing the same things at the same times with the same people. And by all accounts he was quite a happy man."

Charlot scraped her hair back from her forehead with her fingernails but said nothing.

"Makes you think, doesn't it?"

Charlot looked annoyed.

Paul-Henri took a deep breath and continued. "I was curious about why he never married. Not that people aren't allowed to make whatever decision they want, of course, whatever suits them personally, obviously I myself have not—"

"Is this leading anywhere? Paul-Henri, you are making me tired."

He was affronted but stuffed the feeling down out of sight. "Yes, Chief. I spoke to the bank. Of course I couldn't get into his accounts without some permissions, but Alain is an old schoolmate of mine and he took a peek and told me there was nothing out of the ordinary. Belmont was a saver and so his account is actually rather substantial, considering he was a laborer.

"He was an only child and his parents are long dead. I was unable to find out if he had any distant relatives or a will—I have an appointment with André Baudelaire after lunch today, and am hoping he might have something for us on that score. The possibility always exists, I suppose, that some ne'er do well beneficiary is lurking in the wings, looking for an early payout…but obviously that scenario does not, so far, have any facts to support it except that Belmont had a bit of money in the bank."

Charlot put her elbows on her desk and rested her forehead on her hands. "All right," she said. "Next?"

"Number two was visiting Delphus McDougal, an old friend, so he says, from many years ago when they met in Paris as students. Delphus did not admit to any disagreements, said he did not think the victim was anything but happy and enjoying her retirement. She had what he called an illustrious career as a clothing designer and worked for several famous brands. There was no communication from other friends or family during the visit, as far as Delphus knew. He said he wished that we would capture the serial killer before the entire village is in ruins."

"So helpful of him," muttered Charlot. "Next?"

"Number three. From Devon originally, moved to France in the mid-1970s with her family and to Castillac sometime in the 80s."

"Who told you this?"

"Neighbor. And this was the only hint of bad blood I uncovered connected to any of the victims. Miller had a number of dogs—the exact number is in dispute and various friends and neighbors took them in after her death, so it's—"

"I don't care how many dogs she had."

"Right. Yes. I suppose it doesn't—anyway, she had a number of dogs and some few of them were hounds or partly hounds and so they were noisy. According to the next-door neighbor to the south, they howled all day and all night. According to the next-door neighbor to the north, the dogs were adorable and not that loud. That neighbor took in two of them, one looked like a foxhound and the other one of those little yappy breeds, a Griffon perhaps?"

"I don't care about the dog breeds!"

"Right. So—I suppose we could work on the complaining neighbor, see if the degree of irritation went all the way to thinking the only solution was murder? Cause of death was a heart attack."

"Farfetched, at best."

The two gendarmes sat without speaking. Chief Charlot drummed her fingers on the metal desk, and Paul-Henri stifled another yawn, then stood up. "Well, that's only three. I've got four to go. Do you want me to check them out in any particular order?"

"Do Delphine Bardot, then the rest. I do understand this is far too much for one officer, ridiculous really, and all you can do is skate along the surface—what we are looking for is simply any indication of possible foul play, and then we will zero our efforts in that direction. I will be making the rounds as well. Perhaps someone will tell us different stories."

"Perhaps," said Paul-Henri, who was anxious to leave the gendarmerie and get some fresh air away from Charlot's scowling expression. "Perhaps," he said again, with little conviction that such a thing was going to happen.

※

ANDRÉ WELCOMED Paul-Henri into his small office, offering him a coffee.

"Thank you, I could use it," he said, yanking the hem of his uniform down, something of a nervous habit.

André put the kettle on and measured coffee into a French press. He waited for Paul-Henri's questions but the officer was standing quietly looking at a print on the wall and saying nothing.

"Are you interested in foxhunting?" asked André, referring to the subject of the print.

"What?"

André pointed.

"Oh, dear no," said Paul-Henri. "Excuse me,

I'm experiencing some fatigue. I'm hopeful this coffee will set me to rights."

"I'm sure you and the Chief have been working insane hours, given the...well, what are we calling it? The decimation of Castillac? Serial killer, yes?"

"We have been working very hard, indeed." Paul-Henri took the cup and sat down, inhaling the lovely smell, and gulped nearly the whole thing down at once. "As for serial killer...without compromising the investigation, I can only say...that thus far, there is no evidence for that."

André looked disappointed. "I tried to guess how I might be helpful to you, and I admit, I came up with nothing. So tell me, what can I do for you? I have reached out to a few of the victim's families, offering to do the notaire duties for free. I just...I feel so helpless in the face of what's happening. Didn't know what else to do."

"No doubt the families appreciate it," said Paul-Henri. He took out a small pad and pencil. "This won't take long, I have only a short list to get through." He cleared his throat. "Before his death, had Belmont contacted you, in a business capacity?"

"I never met Belmont." André shrugged.

Paul-Henri sighed. "Well, my list for you is done and dusted, in that case."

André stood. "I'm sorry I couldn't be more

help. Are you—is it all right for me to inquire how the investigation is going? Can you give me anything more specific? People are understandably upset, though I'm sure you and the Chief are doing everything you can—"

Paul-Henri felt and looked more exhausted than he ever had in his life. "Thank you for answering my question. I'll see myself out."

26

A brisk October Saturday, and the routine of Changeover Day was in full swing: Constance had arrived with her usual expostulations and a story about a friend of hers who had been cheated on by her boyfriend yet again, and at what point is it the woman's fault for continuing to believe the pack of lies this man keeps telling her?

"I don't think you can ever say that it's someone's fault they got cheated on," Molly said, putting a bottle of cleaning spray into a bucket. "That's what we call blaming the victim."

"But she's so *dumb*," said Constance. "She has to know that once a cheater, always a cheater."

"People do what they do for reasons," said

Molly. "Even without knowing her, I would bet that being dumb is not the reason."

"Then what is?"

"Oh...something like, she's got it in her head that this man is going to fix all her old hurts. And so if she tells him to get lost, she's letting go of any prospect of salvation from those old hurts. I don't mean she's consciously thinking any of this. But what happened to us in the past—in childhood, especially—it affects the present, whether we know it or not."

"Deep, Molly."

"Far too deep for one cup of coffee and a stale croissant. Do you mind giving the cottage a once-over? I'm taking Rolanda to the market so I'll clean the pigeonnier and we'll just leave together when I'm done. Would you like to join us?"

"Thanks, but nah. Thomas wants to go on a hike. I'm not much of a hiker. But I'm trying to be a good sport."

Molly laughed, imagining (fairly correctly) how this was going to go. "Well, have a glorious time. Make Thomas carry you if you get too worn out."

Constance lit up at the thought of that.

Rolanda's was neat as a pin and there was nothing to clean in the pigeonnier, so the two women headed down rue de Chêne towards the village.

"I'm going to stuff myself silly!" said Rolanda, taking Molly's hand, which pleased Molly and made her feel a little shy.

"What are you looking forward to?" asked Molly. "I usually go to the pâtisserie on Saturdays, but I jumped the gun yesterday and was an absolute pig. Not sure I can show my face in there again today."

Rolanda laughed and they walked in silence for a while, enjoying the cool air and rustlings in the trees.

"Oh, I forgot to ask you—you're looking good, so I guess you got over that illness when you first arrived?"

Rolanda nodded. "Worst stomachache of my life," she said. "I did eat a lot of junk food in the airport—you know how it is, you tell yourself nothing you eat on vacation counts, indulge freely! And so I did. And I guess I paid the price. But all is well now. I went for a long walk yesterday and felt good, and now I want to stock up at the market and start planning the week's excursions. Can't wait to get a tub of that goat cheese!"

"So glad. We'll swing by Lela's first so she doesn't sell out before we get there."

The road was starting to get congested with parked cars as they got to the edge of the village, and the streets were full of market-goers carrying string bags. A few nodded to Molly, she nodded back.

In the front—not the back—of her mind, Molly was thinking about the seven deaths. About how they usually came on Sunday, and so…was something happening on Saturday to put that in motion? Was it merely chance? She told herself to stay alert to anything even slightly out of the ordinary, and then brought her attention back to Rolanda. They chattered about San Francisco's famous sourdough bread and made their way through what was becoming quite an unusually crowded market.

André Baudelaire was talking to Madame Renaud; Molly waved at them but didn't slow down. She saw Lapin buying some sausages from Raoul, saw Manette talking with her hands to a tall, thin man Molly hadn't seen before.

Lela was not in her usual spot, and Molly and Rolanda circled the Place twice looking for her before giving up and going straight to Patisserie Bujold for desperately needed sustenance.

"Bonjour, Edmond," said Molly. "Are you going to be in a mood today or have you gotten over it?"

"I'm sure I don't know what you're talking about," he said, handing a baguette to a short man and taking a handful of coins and sorting them in the register.

"I haven't had nearly enough almond croissants this week," said Molly, grinning.

Edmond smirked and turned to Rolanda, who couldn't make up her mind.

"You can't ever go wrong with an éclair," Molly said. "And of course, the almond croissant—in Edmond's hands—is perfectly sublime."

Rolanda was still gazing into the case, tapping her finger on her chin.

"Well, let's do the Pastry Decision Tree. First question: chocolate, yes or no?"

"Yes."

"Excellent. That narrows the field considerably. Would you—"

"Molly, you're being overbearing," said Edmond. "Just let the woman consider in peace!"

"If you say so, Edmond. Can we have two espressos? And I'll have—"

"I know, seventy-six almond croissants on the double."

"Very funny. I would think you would enjoy my...my..."

"Gluttony," said Edmond with a smile as he started to make the espressos.

"I'm not sure how you stay so slim," said Rolanda, walking a few steps to inspect the last row in the case.

"Slim? Ha!" said Molly.

The doorbell tinkled and in walked Marielle Salomon.

"Bonjour, Marielle," said Molly and Edmond.

"Bonjour," she said, but it did not appear, from her expression, that her day was very *bon* so far. "Do you have the case ready, Edmond? I'm late and had to close the épicerie while I ran down to get it."

"First, let me give you condolences on the death of Belmont, I know he was your close friend. And second, do you not have a delivery boy or some such? That seems the obvious—"

"Oh, don't lecture me," she snapped. "I allowed myself to be pressured into hiring Malcolm Barstow to help out—talk about letting the fox guard the henhouse!—and he was supposed to come at six this morning but no sign of him yet. I don't know why I can't seem to learn to do what my instincts tell me instead of following someone else's advice. Anyway—get me that box so I can hustle back to the store before too many people find the door locked. And thank you about Belmont, it's just...it's unfathomable."

"Pardon me, ladies," Edmond said to Molly and Rolanda.

Molly was chewing on her lip, thinking first about Belmont and then about her friend Malcolm Barstow, whom she believed to have a heart of gold. True, sometimes his behavior was on the sketchy side, but she believed he usually had a decent justification for it. Malcolm had seemed much more settled, of late—more mature, less reckless—and she wondered why he had not shown up for work on time.

※

"Where is Lela, anyway?" a white-haired woman said to Marielle as she hurried back to the épicerie carrying the box of Edmond's pastries.

"I don't know why you're asking me," said Marielle. "She's on the east side of the market, next to the fishmonger."

"I know where her usual spot is, but she's not there!"

"What in the world do you expect me to do about it?" said Marielle, nearly shouting. "Oh, and look who the cat dragged in," she said to Malcolm Barstow, who was leaning in the doorway with his hands in his pockets.

"Funny, I just used that expression on someone else," he said, with a smile so warm it melted Marielle's heart, just a little.

"You were supposed to be here at six," she said. "Take these and set them out nicely on the shelf in the back. Don't leave a lot of crumbs lying around."

Malcolm saluted, took the box, and disappeared down an aisle.

Marielle put on her apron, took a deep breath, and tried to calm down. Everything is all right, she murmured to herself. Everything...is...all...right.

She said the words, but she did not believe them.

Meanwhile, Lapin was bubbling over with excitement, waiting for someone—anyone—to come into his shop. He had brought over the furniture from Lucien Pugh's house, none of it of any interest except for one item, a child's desk. As Lapin imagined saying to people as they admired the desk: people don't go around having beautiful desks made for children unless those people have some real money. *Real* money, he said to himself, grinning.

The desk had been tucked away in a corner of Lucien's small living room, with a curtain hiding one side and magazines piled on top of it so that Lapin hadn't noticed it in his first rushed run-through of Pugh's otherwise meager estate. But once the curtain was pulled back and the magazines removed, he could see that the lines of the small desk were graceful, the cabriole legs ending in a dainty foot. Unusually, it had two drawers side by side with marquetry on the top—jungle animals parading in a sinuous line surrounded by floral garlands. The work was detailed and magnificent, clearly by the hand of a master.

"Bonjour, Lapin!" said Molly, stepping inside with a woman Lapin did not recognize. "Let me introduce Rolanda, who is staying in the pigeonnier. She has an interest in old sticks so I thought you might do."

"*Old sticks?*" said Lapin, starting to be insulted but then remembering the child's desk. "Well, just wait until you see the latest sticks I've got here. From none other than Lucien Pugh, of all people." With fanfare, he led them down the narrow aisle to the desk, which he had polished to a fare thee well. The smell of wax and lemon was in the air.

"Holy moly," said Rolanda, dropping to her knees to look underneath.

"It *is* pretty, if you go in for that sort of thing," said Molly. "A bit fancy for my taste."

"Oh, it's fancy, all right. I've got to get to work on the provenance—I wouldn't be surprised to hear it belonged to…to the Dauphin! Or…Louis *Quinze!* As a child, of course."

"It's *that* fancy?" asked Molly. "Or are you just daydreaming?"

"I most certainly am not." He was too excited to be insulted. "You see, marquetry was fashionable for a time—I'll go into the history in more detail sometime, if you're interested—and so I wouldn't say it is rare, on its own, but this particular piece...look at this jaguar, about to leap! You must admit, it is not something you see every day. And it's going to be worth a pretty penny, I'll tell you that much."

Molly cocked her head. "What was Lucien Pugh doing with a desk like this?"

Lapin waved his hand. "Ah, you'd be surprised how often it happens that something really valuable turns up in an out-of-the-way place. Unfortunately, often we can't trace it back to know how it came to be there. You ever see that American television program, *Antiques Roadshow?* All the time people bring in these things from granny's attic or something they picked up at a garage sale, and it's worth a fortune. And that's in America! Of course there are many, many more treasures here in *la belle France*."

"Owned by the Dauphin?" said Molly, laughing.

"Laugh all you like," said Lapin, grinning.

"He's gonna be laughing all the way to the bank," said Rolanda from under the desk. She was too shy to speak French but she understood more or less what Lapin had said. And she recognized a valuable old stick when she saw one.

Lapin beamed.

"It's got a mark, as you'd expect," said Rolanda, standing and brushing off her knees. "No doubt you saw?"

Lapin nodded, able to understand English but too shy to speak it. He grinned even wider.

"Boulle," said Rolanda, nodding her head and smiling with him.

"I'm afraid you two have lost me," said Molly.

"The French love of bureaucracy is my friend!" said Lapin. "Back in the day, there were guilds and strict rules about verifying furniture, lucky for us. This little desk was made by André-Charles Boulle, an acknowledged master, and the veracity is indisputable thanks to those very rules and regulations which required his mark to be branded on the underside. Take a look!"

"I trust you," said Molly, who though not in advanced pregnancy, wasn't looking for reasons to get on her knees. "Is there anything special you're looking for, Rolanda?"

"Oh, I'm not really shopping."

Lapin's face fell but he recovered quicky. Then he took Rolanda down the next aisle, where he had a few things that just might turn a non-shopper into pulling out her wallet.

Molly, meanwhile, stood rubbing her belly and thinking about what sort of crib she wanted, with the only other intruding thoughts being of lunch, and dinner, and dessert, and then breakfast….

27

Molly woke early Sunday morning and lay quietly in bed, thinking.

Her first thought, as it always was these days, was of the baby—she was still amazed every morning when the reality of it set in; it was like getting the best present on earth, day after day. As she kept doing all day long, she put her hands on her belly, wondering when she would be able to feel it moving. Nothing but a slight gurgle of hunger.

And what else? The German couple had arrived, their English was perfect, and they were happily ensconced in the cottage. Saturday night's dinner, home with Ben, had been roast lamb, one of his specialties, deeply satisfying and delicious. Frances and the baby were doing well, with Luka sleeping a little better lately.

But...there was that insistent tickle in the back of her mind. Something trying to get her attention. Something she wasn't noticing that she needed to notice.

She kept running down the list, kept expecting something jarring to pop up, her anxiety building.

And finally, having woken up thoroughly at last, she worked out what it was: it was *Sunday*. The day that Castillacois had tended to drop dead of late. Sunday was when she got news of the deaths, one by one, except for Delphine Bardot.

The thought of that long list of Sunday tragedies made her want to hold her breath all the way until the day passed, praying that this Sunday would be an end to it.

Molly slid out of bed and went to make coffee, Bobo leaping around as though it were doggy Christmas.

"What has got you so worked up?" she said, squatting down to pet her, her body creaking a little from the pregnancy. "I don't have any special treats. If you're thinking about that roast lamb, you can just forget it, I'm having it for lunch. Or maybe I won't wait that long."

A sleepy Ben appeared and she went to him, wrapping her arms around his neck and grinning.

"I've got to throw down some coffee and get going," he said. "Surveillance."

"Ah, too bad. I've got a long list of things planned today. The first is: lie in the meadow and look up at the clouds. And the rest are along the same lines."

He drank his coffee, kissed her on the neck, and was gone. Then he stuck his head back in the door to ask if they were having dinner at Chez Papa that night, their usual Sunday custom.

"I don't know," said Molly. "You know it's Death Day, right? If someone else dies, and we show up there..."

"Yes. I know."

"Well, let's see how the day goes. Hopefully, this Sunday won't be like the others."

Molly held up both hands with fingers crossed, they kissed goodbye again, and Ben took off.

※

THAT NIGHT, Chez Papa was packed. The mood was...funereal.

"Nico," said Frances, leaning next to his ear, "what do you think about giving out some free drinks? People are *morose*."

"I can't do that without Alphonse giving the okay. And he's been home sick for months, I don't want to bother him."

"Well, what can we do? Maybe I should do a little soft-shoe on the bar?"

Nico laughed and went back to the other end of the bar to take some orders.

"Where's Molly, that's what I'd like to know," said Lapin, loud enough that people in the crowd turned and murmured.

Frances narrowed her eyes at Lapin. "Well, is it any wonder she's not here, with all the pressure everyone is putting on her? You'd think she was responsible for the whole mess herself!"

"Now that's just silly," said Lapin. "You're such an exaggerator, Frances."

Frances glared. Her glare was potent but Lapin was unmoved.

"Has anyone heard anything?" asked Anne-Marie. "It's Sunday night already, maybe...?"

Frances jiggled Luka in the baby carrier and squeezed her feet, then shrugged.

"Nothing so far," said Lapin. "Though the night is young. Let me get you a round of drinks," he said, motioning to Anne-Marie, Frances, a man he'd never met, and Lawrence, who had just come in and squeezed in next to the bar.

"Excellent!" Lawrence said. "And in answer to

that question—no. No deaths today. As of fifteen minutes ago, at any rate."

"It almost feels too much to hope for," said Anne-Marie.

"That is unusually dark, for you," said Lapin.

Anne-Marie shrugged. She only felt the way much of the village felt, and she wasn't going to pretend otherwise. "So honestly? For a bit more darkness? What I'm thinking about this whole thing ... so what if what we're all fervently hoping for comes to pass, and Sunday comes and goes without a death. Does it really mean anything? Maybe simply that our serial killer is simply taking a day off. Maybe he'll make up for it and kill two people next Sunday. Or maybe he's got an idea to switch days, and the deaths will start coming on Wednesdays."

Lapin looked aghast at Anne-Marie, his mouth hanging open.

"I understand. I mean—the feeling of hopelessness," said Frances. "But I'm going to try to keep from sinking all the way into the darkness with you. Just consider: you may be right about the serial killer changing things up. But it's equally possible that Sunday is going to pass with no one dying, and that will be the end of the streak. For good.

"Obviously I have no idea whether we'll ever

find out what's been going on. Maybe nothing at all, maybe it's just a statistical bad run as Molly and Charlot have said. I'm going to have a dish of hot frites and think about something else. My life is chock-full of fascinating things like what kind of diaper is best, baby food, and stain removers—so I'm going to think about those instead."

"Not like you to retreat from reality," grumbled Lapin. "Everyone is acting out of character and it's unsettling."

Since handing out free drinks wasn't an option, Nico figured music was worth a try. He didn't mind drowning out conversations because from what he'd overheard, all the conversations were grim. He put on a CD of disco music and turned it up as loud as it would go.

Thankfully, some smiles lit up and immediately a few people started dancing. Some scowled, to be sure—but there had already been plenty of that, so Nico felt overall, the strategy was a success. Before long, a line dance had formed and Frances was in the middle of it, holding Luka's tiny hands and moving them to the beat. Lawrence took the opportunity to release all his pent-up anxiety by dancing like a madman.

Lapin kept glancing at the door, hoping to see Molly and Ben stroll in.

Who did stroll in was Albertine, though her stiff and awkward gait would not be described as a stroll. Just inside the door, she stopped in her tracks, scowling. She shot a dirty look at the dancers, put her hand on the door as though about to go right back out.

But instead she paused and took a deep, ragged breath. Then she walked—stiffly, awkwardly—straight to Lapin and rapped his chest with her fingers.

"Albertine," said Lapin. His voice was kind. "What can I do for you?"

She leaned up to speak in his ear. "I know about the desk," she said. "Don't think for one minute you're going to get away with it."

"Get away with what? Lucien's nephew Tom has entrusted me to take care of the estate. Everything in the Pugh house is under my purview. I don't know what you're going on about."

Albertine narrowed her eyes at him, then spat on his shoe.

Lapin's eyes bugged. "What in the world—?!"

Albertine turned and walked—stiffly, awkwardly—out of the bistro.

"Did you see that?" Lapin said to Anne-Marie, who had been dancing next to him.

"What?" said Anne-Marie.

Lapin just shook his head and shrugged. He didn't feel like dancing and didn't understand how anyone could. And he had known Albertine since she was a child—her ways had always been mysterious, so why bother trying to work out the whys and wherefores?

Hours passed. The dancing went from exuberant to ragged, many people went home, the frites ran out. Eventually Nico changed the music to Bach and turned it down low.

"It's late," said Frances. "How long are you staying open?"

"In a village crisis like this, as long as people want me to," Nico said. "If you want to go put Luka to bed, go ahead, I'll be home when I can."

Frances was tired but she didn't want to miss out on any news—in her mind, she was acting as Molly's lieutenant, gathering information while her superior was otherwise engaged. Though admittedly, at past one in the morning, so far there had been no information to gather.

"Hey," said Lapin, rousing himself. "It's technically Monday. No one died."

"That we've heard of," said Anne-Marie.

"This dark direction you've turned in—I'm not in favor," said Lapin.

"I'm going home to bed," said Frances. "And

I'm going to wake up later today and expect that the body count has not budged."

"That's the spirit!" said Lapin, clapping her on the back a little too robustly.

Luka startled and burst into tears, and the truth was, everyone who remained at Chez Papa felt an urge to join in the sobbing.

28

"You could simply have come to my office, or I to yours," said Florian grouchily, as he and Chief Charlot settled onto a bench in the Place.

"I wanted to speak to you privately," said Charlot.

"It's a little cloak and dagger for Castillac."

"Hardly. We're simply sitting on a bench, for heaven's sake. I did not ask you to don a disguise."

Florian crossed his arms. His mind was on Selma, as it usually was, only this time slightly less morosely, as he had gotten an email from her that morning. No promise to return, but the tone was at least warm. "Well, what's on your mind? No doubt you were cheered by the passage of Sunday with no deaths—at least, none that have been discovered so far," he added, just to give the Chief a dig in the ribs.

"Yes. I'm sure we all felt relief." Charlot stuck her legs straight out like a grade-schooler, then crossed them under the bench. "I don't need to point out that the whole business of deaths coming on Sundays matters not at all, and is nothing but pure random chance—that is, if your conclusions about the victims are legitimate."

Florian held out his palms and shrugged. He was oh so tired of this conversation, around and around, the same thing, natural or foul play, foul play or natural. He was entirely over it.

"The designations of cause of death, in each instance, were not a near thing, Chantal. Not something I was concerned about, in the sense of thinking perhaps I was mistaken because it could go a different way. What I'm saying is: the cause of each death was —every single one—clear cut. Obvious. Nothing contradictory, nothing confusing. Matthias could have done it. A child could have done it. The signs, both pre- and post-autopsy, were unmistakable."

Charlot said nothing. She lifted her feet up again and then tucked them back under the bench.

"People seem to *want* them to be murder victims. It's made me *persona non grata*, you know," he said.

"Join the club."

Florian thought of the way the light in the pigeonnier had played on Selma's rosy skin, how she had hopped up and down with excitement when he came through the door after sneaking away from the office, her full-throated laugh.

"I do hear what you're saying," said Chantal. "But—no insult intended, I'm only being thorough—I want to ask you, again, if you saw any...any little thing, any anomaly, that gave you even a nanosecond's pause. Don't get defensive—I am not disputing what you have reported and the conclusions you have reached. I am only trying to understand whether there could be something... something tying all these deaths together, that so far we have not seen."

Florian did not answer but made no move to leave.

"Make it make sense," Charlot said in a low voice, and Florian could hear the despair in it.

ON MONDAY, Molly was at loose ends, with Ben at work and her German guests being independent sorts with their own plans for seeing the local sights. Aimlessly, she got on her beloved scooter and went into the village, thinking maybe Frances and Luka would like to do something.

Frances and Luka were taking a nap. Lapin was busy with three customers. She dropped into Patisserie Bujold for a fix; the almond croissant hit the spot as always, but Edmond was busy with a repairman and semi-hysterical over one of his ovens that was baking too hot.

She went into a shop that carried baby things—a shop she had avoided ever since she arrived in Castillac—and looked at the cribs and strollers for a moment. But with an apology to the clerk, Molly was soon back on the street. It wasn't time for nesting, not yet. And as much as she kept telling everyone that all she wanted to do was focus on the baby—exactly how was she supposed to do that with seven villagers dead in a matter of weeks?

Molly climbed back on the scooter and contemplated, unused to being at such a loss for company or something to do. It wasn't so much standard loneliness as a feeling of bated breath, of waiting for the next bit of bad news, when being with a friend would be reassuring.

Well, nothing like whipping along a twisty road on the scooter to brighten a mood, she thought, and sped out of the village with the cool air in her face. Helmet on, of course, and not quite as fast as usual.

The road was narrow and curving. Trees were starting to lose more of their leaves, and she could see farther into the forest. The ferns were dying back, the colors were all shades of brown with a bit of faded green. She passed two bicyclists and a woman walking with a staff and a backpack.

Eventually, without consciously intending to, Molly reached Lela's goat farm and turned onto the dirt road leading to the house. Might as well pay a call, see how she's doing, thought Molly, knowing that Lela lived alone and might need someone to check on her.

And in fact, Lela was not doing well at all.

29

Back at La Baraque, Molly went straight to the computer and googled. She clicked through website after website until she found what she was looking for. Then she searched for confirmation, and found it. She shook her head slowly.

People aren't going to believe this, she thought. Then she sat back in her chair, hands on her belly, fingers tapping, as one by one, she considered each victim in turn.

Just last summer she had had reason to consult with Chloe, the accomplished herbalist in Bergerac. The two of them had put their heads together for some hours, and Molly had come away with a new appreciation for the good—and bad—that plants could do. She was a longtime gardener, if mostly a lapsed one; she kept intending to start a medicinal herb garden under Chloe's instructions.

What she was researching now was anything but medicinal. People think of plants as being so good, so healthy, so innocuous! Oh, sure, there's poison ivy, but that's not going to kill anyone, right? Socrates drank hemlock, okay, that one's pretty bad…but the general sense people have, Molly thought, is that plants are good. And so maybe that is why Lela never realized, Florian never considered, certainly not Chantal or Paul-Henri—for of course botany was not part of training at the gendarmerie—no one who has been working to understand the seven deaths ever thought, even for a moment, about the goats.

꧁

THAT NIGHT, Ben returned to La Baraque exhausted from the effort of watching nothing happening. He got a beer and flopped down on the sofa, telling Molly in some detail about all the nothing that had happened, until he noticed that Molly looked like she was about to burst.

"What is it?" he asked. "Is something wrong?"

"No. Not at all. I think…I haven't told—I wanted to talk to you about it first—but I think I have finally figured it out."

"Figured *what* out?"

"What's killing everybody!" She did a little two-step and waved her hands over her head, grinning.

Ben's eyes got wide. "Well, go ahead then!"

"Okay, so, listen with your most critical ear and tell me if I've gone wrong anyplace."

Ben nodded.

"So...to tell the story from the beginning: roughly three weeks ago, people started dying. Every Sunday. Natural causes, according to Florian. Everybody was jumping on him for being wrong, and jumping on me to catch the serial killer...but I'll tell you, the older I get? The more I believe intuition is gold. It's what we should always listen to, always look to first when trying to work out any sort of problem."

She paused and Ben could barely stop himself from shouting at her.

"My intuition was telling me that the villagers were wrong, there was no serial killer—that these Sunday deaths weren't happening because some evil person among us was trying to murder everyone in Castillac one by one. Now, the problem of course was that I had no idea whatsoever what *was* causing the deaths. I had no alternative explanation. I figured—along with Chantal—that it must be just random, nothing more than a statistical anomaly. But that was only my fallback position because I had no other ideas.

"Maybe that was lazy of me. Maybe I was feeling a little tired of death and wanted to lollygag through the happy days of this pregnancy, feeling as little stress as possible." She shook her head. "Tell me: would you call goats nefarious?"

"Goats? I don't follow."

"The first Sunday that passed without a death was also the only Sunday when Lela was missing from the market on Saturday."

"You don't think Lela—"

"No, no, of course not. But the Sunday pattern of death was curious, don't you agree, and that pattern being broken the very same week Lela wasn't there...I mean, for sure it could have been chance. Meaningless. But it gave me pause. And now...I don't think it was meaningless at all.

"I went to see Lela today. She's home, still recovering from a nasty bout of the Hershey squirts."

"The what?"

"American slang for diarrhea. Lela was having some fairly serious gastrointestinal problems and had just gotten back from the doctor. She looked like hell, to be honest."

"Same as death number six. The gastro problems, I mean."

"Right. Exactly! This is what I think happened:

SEVEN CORPSES ALL IN A ROW

Lela was poisoned by eating her goat cheese, and so were the others. Not because the milk was contaminated, or anything like that. It's not a bacterial thing, not a question of sanitation, even though you might think so because of the diarrhea. The cause, I believe, is so much more interesting. The goats—starting just before the first death—had been turned out in a new pasture, and this new pasture has *colchicum autumnale*, a pretty little crocus, growing in it, along the fence. The plant is quite toxic and can be fatal to humans if eaten. It doesn't bother the goats—they can notoriously eat anything, even tin cans, if the cartoons I grew up watching are true—but the plant toxin gets into the milk, and then you end up with poisonous cheese."

Ben shook his head. He took a big glug of his beer. They sat looking at each other. Ben burst out laughing. "You mean the entire village has been suspecting everyone else of methodically killing off their neighbors...and it was actually the *goats?*"

"Yes!"

They enjoyed a moment of relieved hilarity, reveling in the way the world could sometimes be so unexpected and ridiculous. "Of course, we'll need to have the cheese tested to be sure. But from talking to Lela, then taking a quick wander around that pasture, and just a wee bit of googling, it appears to be a likely explanation."

"You saw this poisonous plant in her pasture?"

"Yes, I went back to look once I had the idea. Just a few days ago, I went over to watch the dog—we had a conversation about her pasture, and what the goats like to eat. I didn't see the crocus then, and of course Lela hadn't noticed it on the border of her pasture. It's not difficult to identify if you know what to look for. But also—it's also not showy, when not in bloom. It blends in easily if you're not looking for it specifically. So I can see how Lela wouldn't have had any idea."

"How in the world did *you* know what to look for?"

Molly shrugged. "Chloe got me interested in poisonous plants. It was just something I read about sometime."

"You have strange reading habits."

"Look who's talking, Mr. Napoleonic Naval Battles."

Ben kept shaking his head—he believed Molly, but at the same time, the entire story was unbelievable. "So has Florian lost his mind? I mean, I understand that this might be a novel cause of death that he hadn't seen before. But how could he be wrong seven times in a row?"

"No, that's the funny thing. He wasn't wrong

about any of it—the actual causes of death are just what he said they are. But—the exacerbation of those conditions, the spark that lit the fire, I guess you could call it 'the cause of the cause'—that was the poison in the crocus."

Ben was stroking his chin, then pursing his lips. Molly recognized these movements as something Ben did when he had something to say that he didn't want to say.

"But Molly," he said finally, "sure, number six died of gastrointestinal distress. But what about the others? Heart. Kidney. Liver. I'm not seeing…"

"I know, on the surface it doesn't seem to work. There are doubtless a lot of villagers—Lela's customers from the last weeks—who ate the cheese and had stomach upset and recovered, just as Lela seems to be doing. For more confirmation, we'll have to ask around about that. It's just occurring to me this moment—it might be what made Rolanda sick! She was eating that cheese only minutes after arriving in Castillac.

"Anyway, I'm willing to bet that all the victims started out with diarrhea and a stomachache, and then, things went from bad to worse. People are physically so different. Our bodies have different strengths and different weaknesses. So if someone's kidneys were already struggling—and they may have had no symptoms, may have had no idea at all that was the case—the poison could make those languishing kidneys fail. In someone else, the poison might tip the scale for their heart.

"Another way to explain—imagine someone's health is declining, but she doesn't feel that bad, she says to herself she's just getting older, some aches and pains are to be expected—or maybe she doesn't even have symptoms—yet something inside is starting to go wrong. There's weakness of metabolism, of some organ. Picture these people walking along a cliff, but they don't realize the precarious position they're in. And it could be almost anything—a virus, say, or a fall. A terrible emotional blow. Or—"

"Or some goats eating crocuses—"

"—or some goats eating crocuses. And that amount of toxicity, in healthy people, wouldn't kill them. Maybe wouldn't even make them terribly sick. But if you're already walking along the cliff…"

Ben just sat, shaking his head. "You are a wonder, Molly Sutton."

"I'm quite happy you think so," she said, beaming, and they fell into a soft and loving kiss.

"And even though I certainly hope I am not walking along one of those cliffs, I'm so grateful I lost the cheese I bought when Rolanda and I went to the market. That pregnancy absent-mindedness came just at the right moment."

Ben nodded emphatically. "Have you told Lela about this?"

"I didn't work it all out until I got home and could do a bit more research. She had bought some new land from a neighbor, so that's why this hasn't happened before—the colchicum was on the neighbor's land, not hers. Planted by his late wife, apparently. I called Lela once I had the theory. She's horrified, of course. Feels responsible. I asked another neighbor to go keep her company for now."

"The cheese is not for sale in any stores?"

"No. Now if you're in agreement, we should call Chantal so she can take over getting the word out?"

"Yes. Call her right away. That is going to be a phone call she will be very, very happy to receive."

Molly nodded and started to tap the number for the gendarmerie.

III

30

Madame Renaud's kitchen was spotless. She regularly pulled the oven and refrigerator away from the wall to clean behind and under them, so the kitchen was clean even in places you could not see.

"Gilbert, thank you for washing your dishes. You're becoming a responsible young man."

Gilbert was happy to hear this, because the closer he got to manhood, the closer was freedom from his suffocating mother. He thought maybe now, in this moment while his mother was pleased with him, was a good time to ask her a question that had been hovering in his mind for weeks.

"Maman," he said, his voice smooth. "Did you

hear about Molly Sutton? How she figured out Lela's goats were poisoning people?"

Madame Renaud pursed her lips, then gave a quick nod.

"I don't understand why you don't like her. Just think of how many lives she just saved!"

"I don't believe seven deaths is anything to brag about."

Gilbert made a face. "You are twisting up the facts, Maman. That all happened before Molly figured it out! Why can't you give her credit when she does such amazing things?"

Madame Renaud shrugged and took a cloth and wiped the already clean kitchen table.

"Did you put on clean socks? It's nearly time for the bus. You can't learn anything if your socks aren't clean."

Gilbert rolled his eyes.

"And don't be rolling your eyes at me, young man. It's disrespectful."

"Well, I think it's disrespectful not to give Molly Sutton credit after what she just accomplished. It could have gone on for weeks and weeks and weeks! We could have had a pile of bodies in Castillac as tall as...as...the Eiffel Tower!" he finished, wishing he could have thought of a more interesting comparison.

"I prefer an aged cheese to that nonsense Lela sells," said his mother.

Gilbert was a little too young to know how to respond to such a deflection, and stood with his mouth open, mind working, still regretting "Eiffel Tower."

He had wanted to ask his mother if it was all right if he went to see Molly after school. Maman had never allowed him to pay her a visit though Molly had invited him numerous times.

Clearly his mother was not going to give permission. If Gilbert wanted to see Molly—and with this new case solved, he wanted to, desperately—he was going to have to do it on the sly.

※

"It's the woman of the hour!" said André, grinning at Molly and motioning to Blanchefleur to go inside La Baraque ahead of him.

Molly turned a light pink. "Thanks," she said. "Lucky fluke, really."

"Bonsoir, André, bonsoir Blanchefleur," said Ben, kissing cheeks and then taking their coats. "Come in by the fire, it's chilly tonight."

"I must tell you, I'm greatly impressed with your detective work!" said Blanchefleur. "How in the world did you realize it was the goats!"

"Such intelligence she has," said André, winking at Molly. "Seriously, you could give all those whiz-kid technology types a run for their money. You really know how to add two plus two and get the whole enchilada!"

Molly thought she understood what he was getting at, and smiled at the compliment. "Well, we won't be serving any goat cheese canapés with your aperitifs," she said.

André and Blanchefleur laughed and came into the living room, where Ben handed them kirs.

They all sat. A moment of awkward silence, since their friendship was only at its beginning. Molly noticed that Blanchefleur was looking vacantly at the rug, as though she were a million miles away.

André took Blanchefleur's hand and squeezed it. "All right, love?" he murmured to her.

Blanchefleur nodded, but Molly could see tears in her eyes.

"All right if I talk about it?" André murmured, and Blanchefleur nodded again.

"It's…well, hope you don't mind my jumping into something so personal, when we've barely sat down," said André. "But…these recent events have stirred up…not that it was put to rest, in any case… it's…"

Blanchefleur looked at André with a warm

smile. "What he's trying to say is that recent events here in Castillac—in short, all the death—it has been very hard for us, for André and me. I don't mean to say that the two of us are special, or anything like that. But...when your spouse dies unexpectedly, it makes death—it makes you...sensitized, maybe? Or is it traumatized? I don't really have the words."

Molly and Ben were nodding.

"I knew about your wife's passing, obviously," said Ben, looking at André. "And I'm sorry about your husband, Blanchefleur. It was unexpected, your husband's death?"

She nodded, eyes filling up with tears.

"That's obviously been part of what's allowed us to become so close, so quickly," said André. "When Marianne fell on that hiking trip, and shockingly did not survive, it was just so...so terribly lonely. Like part of myself died with her. It's not the same as a friend dying, or even a parent. It's...it's something no one can understand unless they've been through it. One of those clubs you wish you weren't a member of."

Blanchefleur smiled and put her arm around him.

"I'm so sorry for you both," said Molly. "And I suspect—that people probably *really* don't want to think about such things and might even have avoided you after it happened. I mean, after the funeral. Like they want to think everything snaps back to being just the same."

"Yes!" said Blanchefleur. "It can feel almost as though people think death is catching, and they better stay far away from you."

All four of them took sips of their kirs, contemplating.

"Well, then!" said André. "On to happier subjects. Is it all right to ask some questions about the goat cheese case? Because we are *brimming* with questions!"

Molly shrugged, feeling a little embarrassed.

"Tell us about this poison flower," said Blanchefleur. "Maybe because of my name? But the idea of poisonous flowers doesn't sit well with me."

André chuckled. "Nature is fierce," he said. "It can't all be puppy dogs and rainbows."

Bobo lifted her head and growled, and they all laughed.

Molly said, "Oddly, I was just saying the same thing about nature, back when this first started." She went through the story of the poisoned cheese again, from her first surprise at seeing how sick Lela was to her walk around the new pasture, looking for colchicum autumnale.

"You're truly a marvel," said André, shaking his head. "Are the gendarmes painstakingly going through the final days or hours of each victim to make sure they actually ate the cheese?"

Molly cocked her head. They ought to be, she thought, but didn't want to say so out loud. "Seems like it would be standard police practice?"

"Molly, I haven't even congratulated you on your good news," said Blanchefleur. She looked at Molly's belly, which was how Molly understood that Blanchefleur was talking about her pregnancy. "I have a son—he's the absolute light of my life, as probably all mothers say." She laughed.

"He's at Saint Anselm's. Fantastic school," said André.

"That's boarding?" asked Ben.

"It is, yes," said Blanchefleur. "It was a hard decision for me. But after my husband died, I was in such a state that honestly I did not think it was helpful to Gabriel to live with me. I felt that having some order in his life, surrounded by friends—that might be better than seeing his mother weeping all day and night."

Molly was taken aback. Packed off to boarding school right after your father died? It seemed... well, who was she to judge? People do different things for all kinds of reasons, she reminded herself, always trying to keep her naturally judgmental nature in check.

"Everything was—it was just so sudden,"

Blanchefleur said, almost as though talking to herself. "And maybe I sound terribly shallow, but at least my husband had put away plenty of money, so I don't have to worry about expenses, or Gabriel not being taken care of if something happens to me. It feels like such a responsibility, being the lone remaining parent."

Molly nodded. "You feel anxiety about your own death, having gone through your husband's? Makes perfect sense."

"Yes, it's the same for me," said André. "I'm terribly afraid of heights now, after what happened to Marianne. I'm seriously the biggest chicken alive, can barely look out of a second-floor window!" He laughed. Blanchefleur tightened her arm around him. "These big things…they change our lives forever," he said, looking down at the rug, and then shrugging.

They went in to dinner soon after, and their conversation turned to lighter subjects; there was much laughter and Molly went to bed that night once again grateful for having moved to Castillac and for her rich life there. Bobo stopped sounding grouchy and hopped up on the bed with Molly and Ben, and since the night was cold, she had the thrill of being allowed to stay the whole night long.

31

Milo Clavel smoothed back his scruffy hair, which appeared to have a cowlick running straight down the middle of his head from front to back, and after the smoothing, it sprang right back up again.

It was lunchtime, and he was hungry both for food and female companionship. The center of Castillac in the middle of the day was hardly a prime cruising location, but Milo was used to making do with less-than-optimal conditions. And his standards were not high, in any case.

A young woman came around a corner holding a bag from Patisserie Bujold. She looked to be in her late twenties and entirely out of Milo's league.

"Hola," said Milo, nonchalantly leaning against the back of a bench.

"Oh, so you're Spanish now?" The young woman laughed.

"How do you know I'm not?" said Milo, walking towards her.

"Because I know who you are. I know exactly who you are."

"I do have a bit of fame around these parts."

The young woman hooted. "Fame? Is that what you call it?"

"How about we continue this lively discussion over some lunch—my treat. La Metairie, perhaps?"

"You couldn't afford La Metairie, Milo."

He pulled a wad of euros out of his pocket enough to show her, and then stuffed them back in his pocket.

She raised an eyebrow. "Who'd you steal that from?"

"You're calling me a thief, and we've never even met."

"One thing has nothing to do with the other."

Milo couldn't think of anything to say to that. He liked it much better when women were sweet and placating. If she knew of him, surely she would know he was grieving, after suffering the terrible, terrible loss of Delphine. Was he to get no sympathy whatsoever?

He walked past her, trying to think of a clever insult, but came up with nothing, and decided that he would go to Patisserie Bujold. He would buy himself a massive bag of pastries and eat them all himself, and that stupid girl could just go to hell.

"If you're expecting a brass band and champagne corks popping, just forget it," said Paul-Henri as Molly stepped inside the gendarmerie.

Molly laughed. "You're talking about the goat cheese?"

"Of course I'm talking about the goat cheese." He paused. "It was quite a stroke, I'll give you that."

"Appreciate it," said Molly. "Is Chantal around?"

"Chief Charlot is out on official business," said Paul-Henri with a sniff.

"Mm. Well, I was wondering…actually, to give credit where it's due, André Baudelaire was wondering whether all the recent victims are being checked, to see whether they definitively ate the toxic cheese."

Paul-Henri was not the best at hiding his feelings, and just then his feeling was alarm. "Certainly," he said.

Molly did not believe him for one second. Of course, Chantal might be out of the office doing that work without keeping Paul-Henri in the loop, but wouldn't she have put the junior officer on the grunt work?

Admittedly, Molly had a little spring in her step at the prospect of having some investigating to do, even if it there was nothing pressing about it now that the cause of the deaths was already nailed down. More a matter of dotting those final i's. She waved goodbye to Paul-Henri and went to get her doctor's appointment out of the way.

Molly did not have a good relationship with the village doctor, Francois Boulet. They had a bit of unpleasant history, and apart from that, she just plain didn't like him. But so far—out of laziness, admittedly—she hadn't yet found anyone to replace him.

And now she was supposed to be seeing a doctor every month to check on her pregnancy, so she arrived inside Boulet's office with the kind of attitude one might have when doing something one really doesn't want to do but must.

"Malcolm!" she said, coming into the tiny waiting room. "Are you all right?"

"Sure, sure," said Malcolm. "How's Ben? How's that little bean?" he said, pointing at her belly.

"All well," said Molly, smiling at him.

She was curious. "So…is your mother all right?"

Malcolm nodded.

"What are you doing here, then?" she blurted out.

Malcolm simply smiled.

"You do like keeping your cards close to your chest, don't you?" she said.

"Long habit," he said.

Just then Daisy came out of the exam room. She startled at the sight of Molly, then looked down at the floor and went straight to the door.

"See ya," said Malcolm over his shoulder, as he followed Daisy out of the office.

The door banged shut and Molly stood looking at it, thinking. But she reached no conclusions or anywhere close. It's curious, she thought, several times, but made no headway at all.

32

December 1975

THE CHILDREN WERE noisy in the *cantine*, not shrieking but simply full of high spirits as it was the Christmas meal, the last before school let out for the holiday; they were excited about the feast as well as the impending visit from *Père Noël*. They were not little children any longer, but edging toward the unsettling world of teenagehood—but Christmas is Christmas.

A few had already made it past the chasm of puberty: Delphine Bardot, looking older than her age, her figure curvaceous and her mien regal as she presided over a long table as the other students were digging into their hors d'oeuvres: a small pile of gougères and a deviled egg.

Marielle Salomon sat on one side of her; Solange Forestier on the other. The three were giggling over something Albertine had done in history class.

Albertine was seated at the end of the long table, her long braids lank and threatening to sweep into her plate. Her head was bowed as though she were praying, but prayers were not what was on her mind.

What she was thinking was: Solange and Marielle and most of all Delphine deserve to fall down a flight of stairs and crack their heads open.

Well, it was a sort of prayer, though perhaps not to God.

"Let Albertine alone," said Delphine. "What about that shirt *le prof* was wearing today in English? I don't think my eyes will ever recover." She laughed, and the sound of her musical laugh made students at other tables turn to look at her.

Just then Iris Gault came out of the kitchen, carrying a tray with an enormous *bûche de noël*, so heavy she could barely carry it. The *bûche* was complete with candy mushrooms, holly leaves of icing, and even a little marzipan squirrel sitting on top holding a walnut between its paws.

The room gasped, then burst into applause.

As lovely Iris walked past Albertine, she looked down at the girl with a kind smile. But Albertine responded by sticking out her foot and tripping Iris. The tray lurched; the bûche de noël went up in the air and then, in seeming slow motion, flopped onto the floor with a deflated squishy sound.

The room froze for a moment.

It was all Iris could do, in those next moments, to keep the students from giving Albertine a thrashing—or worse—once they realized it was she who had ruined their lovely cake.

And for what?

33

The next morning, Molly waved Ben off to his surveillance job with a kiss and a few murmurs of sympathy because the job was so boring, then wasted no time hopping on the scooter and heading into the village. First stop: the coroner's office.

She sailed in, blew a kiss to Matthias, and plopped into the chair next to Florian's desk.

"I don't know why that chair is there," he grumbled, skipping over bonjour. "Just clutters up the place."

"I see your mood is…not improved," said Molly. "I would have thought—"

"Honestly, there is no requirement for my

mood, in any way, to be the subject of your thoughts. It does not require commentary of any sort, at any time. A person is allowed to be morose if a person feels like it, Madame Sutton. We are not proscribed from emotions just because you wish they were something else."

"I only—"

"—want me to salute you for the discovery about that silly crocus?"

"Silly?"

Florian threw his hands in the air. "Deadly, whatever, call it what you like. And look, here you go—" He lumbered up from his desk and gave her a sharp salute. "You did a good job," he said, without sarcasm.

"Thank you. Stroke of luck really. And isn't it lovely that it provided a solution that also meant your determinations on the seven death certificates were also correct?"

"Extremely lovely," said Florian. He put his elbows on the desk and rested his face on his hands.

"Selma?" Molly said, gently.

He nodded, slowly, his big head going up-up-up and then back down.

Molly waited a moment. She winked at Matthias who grinned back.

"I was wondering…"

"Dear Lord."

"...just whether there might be some record, from your autopsies, which I absolutely trust to have been done one hundred percent by the book...well, my question is: do you routinely inspect stomach contents?"

Florian's eyes had been closed but now he opened one and looked at Molly.

"You want to know if there was cheese."

Molly nodded.

"In fact, I do note stomach contents in an autopsy. But in none of those cases did I find cheese. I expect it had already been digested. We're talking about a soft cheese which would not need to be in the stomach for long. The toxin of colchicum autumnale does act fairly quickly, but it takes some time for the full effects to be felt. Plenty of time for that cheese to be well on its way through the intestines, where it would wreak yet more havoc. And no, to head you off, I do not inspect the insides of the intestines unless I have some particular reason for doing so, which, being ignorant of the circumstances, at the time I did not. Not that it would have mattered, as I just explained, the cheese would not have been in a recoverable form at that point anyway."

"Hm," said Molly, looking down at the floor.

"You want to make sure all seven ate the cheese," Florian said.

"Seems worth knowing."

"You think maybe someone saw which way the wind was blowing, and sneaked a murder in among the crowd?"

Molly shrugged. "It's an idea."

"You think like a murderer."

Molly grinned.

"Thanks for coming in," said Florian, ushering her towards the door, and then leaning against it once she was out, and sighing theatrically.

"Well, of course, Gabriel cheri, I'll send it right away. What was the name again? All right. See you at fall break, can't wait!" Blanchefleur made a kissy sound into the phone and ended the call.

Boys and their candy, she thought, shaking her head but smiling. The students were allowed only one call per week, and what did Gabriel want to discuss? Only a specific brand of candy that he claimed having a stash of would turn him into an instant celebrity and could she please please please send it right away? In all five flavors, and lots of it?

Lots and lots of it?

Again she smiled, grateful to have something so

easy to do that would bring him some happiness. She wondered—as she had daily, sometimes hourly—whether sending Gabriel to St. Anselm's was a mistake. Should she jump in the car right this minute and go fetch him? Was he suffering? Feeling abandoned by his only remaining parent?

She wandered into the bedroom and bent to straighten the bedspread, remembering the night before with André. He was a big man, powerfully built, kind-hearted—and she felt so lucky they had found each other. She turned pink with embarrassment at the memory, though she was only having private thoughts and no one was witness to them.

Perhaps it was a mistake to be staying with him, in his house. It was unseemly, there was no question of that, and the old her—the her from before her husband Louis died—would not have dreamed of staying overnight with a man she was not married to. It was as though, in some way, the death of Louis had washed away her sense of propriety.

But was it washed away entirely? Or did she need to rethink what she was doing, and take a step back? Perhaps she could still date André, but in a more appropriate manner. Or maybe she should go collect Gabriel and take him back to Paris with her, and worry about his education later. And marry André once the dust had settled a bit.

So many decisions to be made, important decisions. They felt impossible to make because she was not the same person as she was before, and the ground under her feet felt rumbly, unsteady, uncertain.

34

Friday afternoon—sometimes it was jumping at the épicerie, with people getting last-minute supplies for last-minute *apéros*, and other times it was completely dead, leaving Marielle with nothing to do but obsess about this or that moment from her past, wondering what it meant, with no distraction of customers and their inevitable problems.

That particular Friday afternoon, just after what Castillacois later called The Slaughter, the streets were almost empty. No one was drifting in to buy a bottle of water or pistachios or just to have a chat. Marielle had sent Malcolm Barstow on a delivery so she didn't even have the dubious pleasure of his company.

Her nerves were on edge.

Understatement of the year.

She stood by the cash register, looking out at the street. She thought about Belmont, and their years of walks together. And she kept thinking about a night back in high school, a night with Delphine, Solange, Manette…the Four Musketeers, their math teacher had called them, one for all and all for one…and that night, the four of them had crowded around Delphine, who had a black eye and it turned out, a cracked rib…

A young girl rode by shakily on a bicycle. Marielle watched her progress, wishing her not to fall, trying to focus on the girl and the bike and not the other, less wholesome thoughts that kept crowding into her mind…Delphine on that terrible night, when she made them all swear never to tell.

The girl managed to get around a corner and was out of sight. Then an old dog appeared from the narrow alleyway between two buildings. It stood blinking in the late afternoon sun, then it sat, scratched an ear. Marielle could see from across the street that the dog's ribs were showing.

Striding down the street with an air of optimism—an entirely different energy than the girl or the dog—came André Baudelaire, a briefcase under one arm, whistling. He was no longer in his prime, thought Marielle, but of course neither was she nor any of the people she had been in school with, and admittedly, André still looked solid, sturdy, and handsome. He had a spring in his step—and more muscle than your average villager.

She watched him stop next to the dog. He reached down to pet its head, she couldn't make out what he said but could see he was talking to the dog. The next minute he was in the épicerie, saying bonjour as he disappeared down an aisle and then reappeared with a can of dog food.

That night she called Solange and told her about how André Baudelaire had fed that hungry dog. And then she had cried herself to sleep over the loss of her friend, Belmont.

THEY HAD GOTTEN some soup from the Cafe de la Place and brought it back to Daisy's, where Malcolm was doing his best to get her to eat it.

"What are you even doing here?" she said, looking up at him through a cascade of black hair that had fallen across her eyes.

"It's simple," he said. "I've had some bad times in my life."

"So?"

"I think you can work it out," he said, laughing. "Eat. Do I have to threaten you with a spanking?"

In normal times this would have made Daisy laugh, as it was intended, but obviously these were not normal times.

She put her hands on either side of her head and rocked back and forth.

"Could you be any more dramatic?" said Malcolm. "I can guarantee that if you eat the soup, you're going to feel better."

"Soup is not going to bring my mother back from the dead."

Malcolm lost patience and stood up.

"I'm a terrible daughter," whispered Daisy.

"Oh, so you're not actually feeling that bad about your mother, it's yourself you're feeling bad about? Guilt getting to you?"

Daisy jumped up, sloshing soup out of the bowl, and pounded on Malcolm's chest. "I killed her!" she cried. "Don't you see? Why are you even here? Take your soup and get out!"

Malcolm looked pointedly at the soup in a puddle on the table, and then waved his hand over his shoulder and left.

35

After a great deal of thinking and arguing back and forth with himself, Gilbert finally decided to ride his bike out to La Baraque rather than walk. He wished to travel in secret, and walking had the great advantage of being able to hop behind a building or a bush if anyone was coming. But on the other hand, it was Saturday, Market Day, and he figured there would be enough people about to make secrecy impossible anyway, and he and his bike would simply blend in with the crowd.

Gilbert had some ideas about being a private investigator when he grew up, which he hadn't told a soul.

His mother's overprotectiveness had taught

him a degree of sneakiness that wasn't natural to him but which he had practiced and rather come to enjoy. And he was old enough to feel that being able to go visit a friend was a right he deserved—that any twelve-year-old deserved—and he was intent on doing it even though his mother specifically told him it was not allowed and he understood he was doing it against her wishes.

He did have some sympathy for her, a woman raising a child alone; he knew it wasn't easy. But what, he reasoned, did that have to do with his freedom?

For a moment, at the beginning of the trip, as he pedaled as quickly as he could to get away from the house and into the village, he felt sorry for himself for having the mother he had. His friends moved around the village easily and without having to report what they were doing every second. But Gilbert shook that feeling off and began to enjoy speeding through the streets. He waved to a classmate, dodged a cat, circled around on the outskirts to avoid the market traffic, and was soon on rue de Chêne, on his way to see Molly.

His legs were strong and he went faster and faster, and soon La Baraque appeared. He saw a rough-looking Renault in the driveway, but no scooter. An orange cat appeared and disappeared like a ghost.

SEVEN CORPSES ALL IN A ROW

Taking one last glance to the road, as though worried his mother might somehow appear behind him, he rapped on the door.

"Well, bonjour, Gilbert, come in!" said Ben, waving him in with a flourish. "Nice to see you."

Gilbert turned bright red. He remembered—suddenly, and quite vividly—that for a long stretch when he was younger, he had nursed a fantasy that Ben Dufort was his father. It seemed ridiculous to him now. They looked nothing alike, for one thing.

"Gilbert? Are you looking for Molly? I'm afraid she's gone to the village, probably she's at Patisserie Bujold as we speak, eating a scandalous number of pastries."

Gilbert felt tongue-tied. He stammered out a thank you to Ben and turned to go.

Then he stopped. "It's just—I wanted to tell her she did something amazing with the poisonous plant and preventing anyone else from dying. I wanted to ask how in the world—"

Ben grinned. "I know," he said. "She's really something."

That memory of hoping Ben was his father bubbled up again and Gilbert said goodbye and hurried off, his face feeling hot with embarrassment as though Ben could read his mind.

He was twelve now. In addition to asking Molly how she had managed to figure out about the poisonous plant, he had wanted to ask her if he could be a sort of junior officer, helping her investigation business from time to time in some way. His mother wanted him to be a farmer and if Gilbert knew anything at all, it was that he was *not* going to be a farmer.

He rolled his eyes and shook his head just thinking about it, pedaling home with a fury.

THE CORONER'S office was not open on Saturdays, though of course if someone died, Florian and Matthias were on call. Florian was at his desk anyway, shuffling papers around and pretending to have something to do.

He checked over the paperwork for each of the recently deceased, considering making an addendum with the information about colchicum autumnale, then deciding against it unless any of the next of kin wanted an exhumation so that he could try to establish whether the plant had in fact been ingested. Putting something in writing that was only likely to be true—that was not how the coroner's office worked.

He spent some long minutes considering what tests might be able to prove ingestion this long after the death.

He googled half-heartedly.

Women are impossible, he thought, for perhaps the ten thousandth time.

We did love each other. I know we did. I know she was not faking it. No one is that good an actress—and in fact, one of Selma's best qualities is that her feelings are always plain on her face. She was not a person who pretended at all, as far as he saw, even when doing so would have made things easier—the way people do, socially, all the time.

Florian had never married, though he had had many girlfriends over the years. He treasured the memory of most of them, even though he had never been tempted to settle down with any of them.

And then, in his fifties, he finally met the woman he desired not just for the moment but for the rest of his life—and *pffft*.

36

Molly returned to La Baraque with a capacious bag of pastries and bubbling energy.

"Coffee eclairs for you," she said, dropping the bag on the kitchen counter. "And let's make fresh coffee, I've got some news. Well, sort of."

Ben's eyebrows went up.

"I talked to Lela at the market. Needless to say, she hadn't brought any cheese to sell. She was just there to answer questions from her customers, which was brave of her, don't you think? Poor woman feels absolutely terrible."

"Understandable," said Ben, measuring the coffee into the press. "How's she going to handle her business now?"

"It's not going to be easy. Of course she put the goats back in their old pasture right away. But obviously, before she can use that new pasture, she's going to have to get rid of every single bit of colchicum autumnale, and so far she's not figured out how to do that without using massive herbicides which she doesn't want to do. She's researching how long it takes for the toxin to leave the goats' bodies. And you know, it remains to be seen whether anyone will trust that the new cheese is safe, no matter what precautions she takes. Or whether any authorities decide to take action, and what that might be."

Ben nodded and put cream in Molly's cup. "I don't want to sound pessimistic, but she's got an uphill climb ahead of her."

"Right. So anyway. As we talked about, I'm trying to see if we can prove that all of the victims ate her cheese. Certainly Charlot should already be doing this and probably she is, but I...I just felt like doing it myself. As a sort of backup, I guess."

"Something feels off to you, am I right? Is it one particular victim you're having thoughts about?"

Molly smiled and kissed his cheek. "Ah, maybe?" she said. "The whole affair just feels a little...unfinished, if you know what I mean. So—Lela doesn't keep records of who bought her cheese, why would she? She only takes cash so there are no credit card records or anything like that. All we've got to go on from that direction is her memory of weeks of sales."

"I'd think it would be very hard to separate one week from the next, especially with so many regulars. And of course someone could have eaten the cheese that someone else bought."

"Exactly. The thing is? Working this out wasn't that complicated. Every person on that list either bought the cheese themselves—usually regulars, who bought cheese every week or two—or were in a household where someone else bought the cheese."

"So case closed then?"

"Let me finish. Every person—but one. Now, that one person could still have eaten the cheese, if, say, she went to someone's house for lunch and ate it there. I was not able to account for every movement this person took—nearly impossible, even in a village this small—but so far...I cannot place one person anywhere near the cheese."

Ben poured the coffee and looked at Molly. "Who?"

"Delphine Bardot," said Molly, shrugging her shoulders. "I'm not saying she was murdered. But as far as I can determine? She didn't eat the cheese."

"Of the seven, she would have been a finalist on my list, if any of them were actually murdered."

"Why do you say that?"

Ben shrugged.

"The others were either from out of town, or not likely to have enemies. I did wonder about Ginette Duchamps, simply because she has money. But I spoke to her housekeeper, Florence, who told me that Madame Duchamps was devoted to Lela's cheese, so much so that Florence had to buy it and deliver it on Saturdays even though Florence didn't otherwise work that day. And by Monday, the cheese was usually all eaten."

"I'll say she was devoted."

"Mm. Well, I still have some more people to talk to, maybe it will turn out that Delphine was chowing down on the cheese too. She died on a Tuesday—the only one not to die on Sunday. But of course that could just mean that she went to someone's house on Monday and ate the cheese. I have to account for all her movements on that Monday. Luckily it's only one day."

THE NEXT MORNING Ben found Molly in the bathroom, looking at herself in the mirror.

"Good morning, beautiful," he said, kissing the side of her neck.

"I am a whale."

Ben snickered, which he immediately wanted to take back.

"I'm not complaining, of course!" she said. "It's just...this whole pregnancy thing...I know, it's the most commonplace thing in the whole entire world, but...when it's happening to you? It doesn't feel commonplace at all. It feels astonishing and wonderful and frankly a little disturbing. Verging on science fiction."

"Are you wondering about boy or girl?"

"Oh, a little. But honestly I do not care one single bit, so it's more like...it would change my vision of the future some? But I don't have a wish either way. Do you?"

"Not in the least."

They stood for a moment, Ben holding her from behind and caressing her gently swelling belly.

"Molly."

"Mm?"

"What are your plans for today?"

"Well, it's Sunday in France, I'm not supposed to have any plans."

He laughed. "The question stands."

"I thought I might...stroll around the village.

See if anyone else is out enjoying the lovely fall day."

"You want to nail down Delphine's movements the day before she died."

She laughed. "Yes, of course, that's exactly what I want to do. But I don't want to be too obvious about it."

"Right." Ben paused. "I admit it's entertaining, watching you do a 180 on the subject of murder. All these weeks, villagers have been pleading for you to take up the case. And ironically, it's only now that you've discovered that toxic cheese was killing people that murder is suddenly on the menu."

Molly laughed. "It does make me seem a little contrary. But the idea of someone killing one or more of the victims was always a possibility, right? I just didn't think…people were all hot on it being a serial killer and I didn't think so at all."

Ben nodded.

"But I'm not—at this point—saying what I believe or don't believe. I'm not being coy. I just think, very simply, with this one victim, we don't yet have a direct link with the cheese. That doesn't mean it isn't there, though."

"For people to talk to—probably that cabal from twenty years ago would be a place to start."

"Cabal?"

"Oh, you know the gang—Solange, Marielle, Manette. They were thick as thieves back in their school days, and I'm sure they were over the moon that Delphine moved back to the village. Or maybe…"

"Maybe one of them, for reasons so far unknown to us…was not so keen?" Molly said softly, and Ben nodded.

※

A LOVELY FALL DAY, with leaves swirling on rue de Chêne and the sun bright, with a brisk breeze that was not too cold. Molly decided, conscientiously, to walk instead of taking the scooter, because as her pregnancy developed, more and more she felt like lying on a chaise with a blanket pulled up to her chin, dozing by the woodstove, and she knew this inclination had to be fought against at least some of the time.

Sundays were never bustling in the village, but people did venture out for walks, and Molly timed her arrival with the hour after the midday meal, hoping to find at least one of the cabal out and about.

She walked down rue Cassis and over to rue Malbec, barely seeing anyone and none she knew well enough to speak to. She swung by Madame

Tessier's but rue Simenon was as quiet as the others. Nothing was open—the pâtisseries and boulangeries were open for a few hours on Sunday mornings so customers could have fresh bread, but those hours were over.

Surprised to be feeling so dejected at seeing no one, Molly finally turned towards home, thinking about the last time she saw Delphine at Chez Papa, and also the first time, when Milo Clavel had been so horrible to her.

Clavel obviously has violent tendencies, or at least dramatic ones, she thought. But the person who murdered Delphine—*if* she was murdered—had to be rather clever. Had to have thought that slipping a murder in when villagers were dropping like flies for some other reason might well keep the murder undiscovered. It was only a fleeting impression—she had never actually had a conversation with him—but she didn't judge Milo Clavel to be that clever. If he killed Delphine, it would be an impulsive thing, not something carefully planned—and the cause of death would have been a knock on the head or something else violent. Not a heart attack.

It was easy enough to cross a suspect off a list, but how to gather any suspects to put on it?

All the way back to La Baraque, she considered Milo Clavel, seeing the scenes of him those two times in slow motion, scrutinizing every movement, the tone of his voice, every detail she could recall. What had Delphine seen in him? There was nothing, not the smallest detail, that made Molly think Milo was anything other than an annoying and rather dimwitted user.

Though how simple the case would turn out to be if she were wrong, she thought, whistling for Bobo when La Baraque came into view.

37

The next morning, Charlot had arrived at the gendarmerie only minutes before Molly was knocking on the door and letting herself in.

"Bonjour, Chantal," Molly said, looking around for Paul-Henri and not seeing him.

The Chief looked drawn. Her eyes had dark circles under them and she looked like she had lost some weight. She narrowed her eyes at Molly. "Bonjour, Molly. What's on your mind?"

"Of course I don't want to be butting in where I don't belong—"

The Chief allowed herself a smirk.

"—but I was doing a bit of poking around, just for something to do, and I just wondered—have you been able to connect Delphine Bardot to the goat cheese? Because try as I might, I—"

"The cheese has been positively connected to all the victims, thankfully. Lela had herself quite a devoted following."

"It *is* superb, don't you think?"

"I can't say. I do my marketing in Bergerac."

Molly gasped.

"What, are you the Mayor? Head of the local business association? Why in the world would you care where I do my marketing?"

Molly took a deep breath. It was so easy to get on the wrong foot with Chantal. "Of course I don't care. Again, sorry if I'm butting in. I was just doing a little match game of who ate the cheese just for something to do. I came up empty with Delphine so I wondered—"

"Yes, that's butting in." The Chief stood up. "Delphine Bardot was at a small get-together on Monday in the early evening where she ate the cheese. So, happily for us all, the case is closed. All accidental deaths. Done and dusted. Finito. If any consequences for Lela Vedal are forthcoming, that is not a criminal matter and not my department. If there's nothing else?" she gestured to the door, and then her posture softened. "Before you go, I do want to thank you for somehow knowing about that poisonous crocus and letting me know. It was quite a strange and bizarre thing, and who knows how many people would have died if you hadn't worked it out. So on behalf of this office, and also personally—thank you."

"You're welcome," said Molly, a little too loud, as she backed out of the door. She wanted to ask where was this get-together Delphine supposedly went to but thought better of it. One minute Chantal despises me, the next she's being gracious. I'm always off balance around that woman, thought Molly.

With the news that Delphine had eaten the cheese—Molly was, no other way to put it, disappointed.

Since she was already in the village, she drove the scooter around to Patisserie Bujold; it had been two whole days since her last pastry. Obviously a lot of other people were feeling similarly bereft and the little store was packed, so Molly waited on the sidewalk, tapping a finger on her chin, thinking about Delphine Bardot.

"Bonjour, Molly!" said a hearty voice, and she looked up to see André crossing the street to talk to her.

"Bonjour, André, *ça va?*"

"Indeed, indeed. It's good to see you, you're looking hale and hearty this morning!"

Molly smiled. "I'm feeling pretty good. No complaints."

André used his hand to block the sun as he gave Molly a good look, cocking his head to one side. "I don't want to be intrusive…but as healthy as you look, you seem…troubled by something? I'm sorry, I'm in the habit of reading people's faces and I should just keep quiet."

Molly shook her head. "No, no, it's fine. You're right. I was thinking…about Delphine Bardot. With all the other victims, it was easy to get confirmation that they did indeed eat the cheese. But with Delphine—I was having a hard time with it."

"Oh dear," said André. "You mean—you think she didn't die from the crocus like the others?"

"Well, just between you and me, I *was* sort of wondering about that. But I've just heard she did eat the cheese after all. I guess my detective skills are a little rusty."

André laughed. "Oh, I doubt that—you are famous, Madame Sutton! You see the underside of life that the rest of us work so hard to pretend doesn't exist!"

Molly patted her belly, thinking about her baby and then about almond croissants, which subjects nearly crowded out any thoughts of this underside André was speaking about. Nearly, but not entirely.

"You know," said André, leaning in so he could speak softly. "I admit, I wondered a little about that as well. Delphine, I mean. Solange Forestier, she's a...well, a funny one, I guess you could say. An academic. Never married. Has a lot of strange ideas about things. And so, with the long history those women had, I couldn't help wondering…"

"Yes?" said Molly, getting interested in spite of herself. "You mean like a…a frenemy situation?" She switched to English, which André was fluent in.

"Frenemy?"

"Friend who's actually an enemy."

André nodded. "Hm, yes. Of course I really have no idea. But…it did cross my mind…whether Delphine was actually alive when Solange arrived that morning. And dead when Solange left. If you see what I mean?"

"The person reporting the death committed the murder? Hiding in plain sight?"

"Exactly."

Molly tapped her chin, thinking.

"Oh, look at me, indulging in silly gossipy day-dreams based on nothing," said André with a laugh. "You'd think I was trying to come up with a plot for a novel. All right, I'm off—appointments lined up all the rest of the morning, I'd better get moving!"

Hide in plain sight, thought Molly, as she went into Patisserie Bujold and inhaled the smell she loved so.

Interesting.

Look at me trying to keep a case alive after Charlot has closed it, she thought. If Delphine ate the cheese, she ate the cheese. I can go back to stuffing myself with almond croissants and finding some roomy caftans to wear.

※

AFTER SCHOOL, Gilbert did his chores as quickly as he could. They included cleaning out the henhouse, which was time-consuming and smelly. And then, in typical twelve-year-old fashion—with no thought of a shower, he leapt on his bike and pedaled away from the house, praying he was fast enough that his mother did not see him go.

Quickly through the village, waving at friends but not stopping, until he was back on rue de Chêne and in minutes careening into the driveway of La Baraque.

Molly was raking leaves in the front yard and walked over with a big welcoming smile on her face.

"I am so happy to see you, Gilbert! Ça va? How in the world did you get away!"

SEVEN CORPSES ALL IN A ROW

He shrugged. He took no pleasure in going against his mother's wishes, even if he was absolutely certain those wishes were wrong and unfair. "Chief Dufort must have told you—I was here day before yesterday?"

"Yes, of course, and remember, he's not Chief anymore. It's Chief Charlot now."

Gilbert rolled his eyes, which made Molly smile to herself.

"Why don't you come in and have some lemonade?" she asked.

"Oh, I can't stay," he said. "But there are two things I want to say. First of all, wow, what a job you did with the poisoned cheese. You're a superstar!"

Molly blushed.

"When I have more time, maybe you could tell me what you're reading, to learn stuff like that. Okay and the second thing is that—" he stopped suddenly, finding it hard to make the words come out of his mouth.

"Yes?" Molly said gently.

"Well, it's...it's embarrassing. But I was wondering, if maybe—now that the cheese thing is all over with and no one else has died and you're hopefully not busy with anything?"

Molly waited. Gilbert's face was strained and she could tell whatever it was meant a lot to him.

"I want to know who my father is," he said quietly. "Maman has always refused to tell me. But I think it's only fair that I should know. I'm not a baby anymore. And I'm half him, right?"

Molly nodded. "You want my help, is that it?"

Gilbert nodded, a lump in his throat.

She knew that saying yes would get her in trouble with Madame Renaud, if she found out, whether or not she succeeded in finding out the information. But eh, Madame Renaud already couldn't stand her, so what was the risk?

"Of course I'll help," she said, unable to stop herself from ruffling his hair. "I can't make any promises, but I'll do my best."

"Your best is superhero level," said Gilbert. And with a nod, he jumped back on his bike and was around the curve of the road before Molly could say another word.

38

"Bonsoir, Marielle," said Solange, kissing her friend on each cheek.

Taking Marielle's hand, Solange led her into the small living room where Manette was drinking a kir.

A silence.

"I miss Delphine," said Marielle quietly. "I know we've had that memorial by the stream and all, but the grief is still fresh and so far, time doesn't seem to be making a dent in it."

The others nodded. Solange raised her glass. "To Delphine," she said, and the others said "To Delphine" in unison.

"How did you get away? Who's holding down

the fort at that zoo you call home?" Solange asked Manette.

Manette shrugged. Solange had been insulting her about the size of her family for years and she paid it no mind. "I feel like we should be doing makeovers," she said. "Remember when we used to do that at Delphine's?"

Solange hooted. "You people made me look like a Russian prostitute!"

"Well, maybe a Russian prostitute with really great makeup," said Manette, laughing.

Another silence.

"I can't help thinking..." said Marielle, and then looked down at the rug.

Manette got tears in her eyes and wiped them away, unembarrassed.

Solange shook her head. "The past is the past," she said. "Now come on, snap out of it! Just cut it out!"

"Emotions aren't evil," said Marielle. "People are allowed to feel things."

Solange scowled. Marielle went back to looking at the rug. "It's just..." she said. "I keep thinking about Delphine's daughter, who's now lost both her parents. And if—"

"If *nothing*," said Solange. "Why go down roads of what-if when we already know the outcome? Look, all right, that whole business? It was literally ages ago. She made us swear we would never talk about it to anyone. Not that we would have dared, given...anyway, the past is finished and the best we can do is forget about it. The whole thing was wrenching and we were all terribly sad—we were young, so that sadness was magnified because we hadn't experienced anything like it before. And even more magnified probably by having to keep it a secret. But none of that has anything to do with now, with this horrible ridiculous poisonous cheese that so unfairly took away our beloved friend."

"Amen," said Manette, still wiping tears.

Marielle drank the rest of her wine in gulps.

"How about this," said Solange. "Since you all insist on being completely undone by this situation—which, to be clear, I miss Delphine too! But how about instead of sitting around moaning and groaning about it, we have a little fundraiser. Just among ourselves, or include anyone else we can think of who might want to participate. And we give Daisy a little something from her mother's old friends. Maybe we could get enough to give her a plane ticket back to New York?"

"You want to get rid of her?"

"I'm only thinking about what she probably wants. She has no ties here, there's nothing for her to do, why in the world would she want to stay?"

The idea of this parentless young woman with

no home or friends made fresh tears roll down Manette's cheeks. The others nodded and murmured agreement.

For the rest of the evening, they talked of other things. But the sorrow was still there, and also, somehow, the fear. Like a suffocating blanket over them all.

39

Within ten minutes of speaking to Annette at the *mairie*, Molly was looking at Gilbert Renaud's birth record. When paperwork was what you needed, France was the best place to be.

Mother: Cataline Renaud, age 29. Father: Jean Moulin, age 33.

Well, that was easy, Molly thought. She thanked Annette, accepted her good wishes for the baby, and was back out on the street in a matter of minutes. The trickiest part of this job is figuring out how to contact Gilbert, she thought. I can't just show up at the Renaud house to deliver the news. I'm sure Gilbert isn't allowed to have his own phone. I suppose he'll come back to La Baraque for an update at some point.

She didn't know any Jean Moulin in Castillac, which didn't mean much. But Molly figured the most likely scenario was that Madame Renaud had had an affair with this man, and when she got pregnant, off he went. Oldest and most unoriginal story in the book.

Before getting back on the scooter, she saw Daisy going into the épicerie. Molly chewed the side of her mouth. She couldn't help…something still felt unfinished, like a dangling thread that needed to be pulled.

Suddenly realizing she had a desperate need for a bar of chocolate—the Cote d'Or with hazelnuts, to be precise—Molly sauntered towards the épicerie, the very picture of nonchalance.

"I DON'T WANT to upset you," Blanchefleur said quietly, lowering her eyes.

"I'm not upset in the least. My little flower, all I ever want is your happiness! And if moving into your own place does that, then by all means, let's arrange it." André kissed her forehead, smoothed her hair, and tucked a bit behind her ears.

"It's just—there's so much…it's hard to say these things, I'm not used to speaking directly. But I haven't been clear enough—it's completely my fault that you don't know this about me, and I can't say why I kept it to myself—but I...the truth is, I'm quite old-fashioned, I guess you could say."

André smiled at her. "This is not a big secret," he said, taking her hand.

Blanchefleur looked relieved. "Really? I'm so glad to hear that! My wanting my own place—it has nothing to do with my feelings for you. Or about how much I've loved our time at your place together. It's only...I have a sense of propriety, you understand? I know it's not modern. My grandmother was a great influence on me and I'm afraid I have taken up her ways of doing things rather completely."

André smiled. "We will look at the listings this very afternoon, and get you settled somewhere lovely. Castillac doesn't have loads of rentals but I'm sure we can find a place that's right for you. And hopefully right around the corner," he added, squeezing her hand.

"Everything in Castillac is right around the corner." She laughed. "And...I know you know this, even though you're not a parent—but I feel, sometimes quite acutely, the pressure of not only doing what is right but showing Gabriel what is right. I cannot be saying one thing and doing another, you understand?"

"Of course, of course," said André. "You must

do what is right for you. And we will be married before long, and then we will start our life together as man and wife, official in the eyes of the Lord, of the state, and of the neighbors!"

Blanchefleur nodded, eyes welling up with gratitude at finding this man who was so accepting of who she was and what she needed. "Right around the corner," she murmured, kissing him with some passion, which he returned with interest.

40

When Daisy came out of the épicerie with a bag of chips, Molly just happened to be right by the door, so that they nearly smacked into each other.

"Bonjour, Daisy," said Molly. "I'm sorry—I know you but you don't know me. I'm—"

"Oh, I know you, all right," said Daisy, shrinking back a little, not smiling.

Molly took a breath and decided to risk it. "I wonder—if you're not doing anything—if I could take you to lunch? Your mother and I were not friends, since I moved to Castillac long after she left and was making a life with you and your father in New York City. So I'm not asking you on that basis. But more because…"

Daisy shrugged her shoulders. She was by this point vexed and fatigued by the constant stream of middle-aged women vying for her attention. It was like they all wanted to have babies again and somehow believed that she, Daisy, a grown woman, could step into that role.

She wanted to shake her head and walk off, ignore this infamous Molly Sutton.

But where would she be walking off to, with her stomach growling so fiercely? She knew better than to buy chips with the little money she had, what had she been thinking?

"Okay," she said, dropping her head.

Molly led her into Cafe de la Place, making a gesture to Pascal to seat them in a corner, away from other diners. They ate some rillettes of duck and then *salades Périgourdine*, Daisy practically lunging at the food. Molly chewed and enjoyed the little nuggets of chicken gizzard, patiently waiting, wanting to see the girl relax just a little before she brought up her mother.

Pascal brought bowls of steaming hot stew, with chunks of parsnip and carrot and beef. Daisy's eyes got very wide and her spoon was in the bowl a fraction of a second after Pascal put it down. He smiled and disappeared into the kitchen.

"Are you feeling a bit better?" asked Molly. "I wonder if anyone is—of course you could use some support right now. Is Malcolm being dependable? I know—believe me, I understand, you're an adult, you can take care of yourself, all that jazz—but you have also just suffered the death of your mother which is one of the biggest stresses we ever go through in our lives. And on top of that...well, not to beat around the bush...I'm guessing money is a problem? Not having enough money—that's another enormous stress, as I'm sure I don't need to spell out for you."

"Yeah, stress," said Daisy with her mouth full. "So what. New Yorkers live on it."

"Mm," said Molly. "I'm just saying...here in the village, we look out for people. It's not like New York. You're not going to sink down out of sight with no one to give you a hand."

Daisy sat up a little straighter now that she had something in her stomach.

"This village is full of middle-aged busybodies," she said.

Molly laughed. "Oh indeed. It absolutely is. I might even claim the title of Chief Busybody."

Then she turned the conversation back to New York, asking the girl questions about what she liked to do there, who she missed, and what places she would travel to if a golden ticket to anywhere in the world dropped into her lap.

In short, Molly circled around the issue of her

mother and whether or not she ate the cheese, and whether or not anyone in Castillac had reason to want her dead.

Molly had a feeling Daisy might know something about at least one of these questions. But she was smart enough, in that moment anyway, not to press for answers.

❧ 41 ❧

It was the most exciting piece to come into his shop in a long, long, time. When Lapin woke up in the morning, it was the first thing he thought of, and when he put his head on the pillow at night, it was the desk he was thinking of as he fell asleep.

That Tuesday, Lapin did everything the same way he did every day of the week. After getting his second coffee at the hole-in-the-wall down the street, he allowed himself to visit the desk, still tucked away in the back of the store, surrounded by much larger—and less valuable—pieces.

He was squatting down beside it, stroking one cabriolet leg with his thumb, when the bell tinkled and he hustled to the front.

"Ah, Albertine," he said, trying to keep the disappointment out of his voice. Lapin loved Castillac; he never once considered moving to a city where the pool of potential customers would be much larger and wealthier—but of course as a consequence he suffered the daily pain of the doorbell tinkling and someone coming in who was never, ever going to spend a single euro in his shop.

Albertine scrunched up her mouth, looked at the floor, and said nothing. Then stiffly walked down the aisle on the right, not looking at anything as she passed by, as though she had an appointment in the back.

"Can I do something for you?" he called after her.

He was expecting an appraiser to come that afternoon to look at the desk. Not that Lapin didn't trust his own knowledge—but it seemed prudent, in the case of something that could be worth as much as that little desk, to call in a second opinion. And to be honest, the prospect of seeing the man's reaction to the desk made his heart sing arias of joyful anticipation.

Lapin was ninety-nine point nine percent sure the man's eyes were going to—as in a cartoon—spring out of his head and spin around while his hair stood straight up. Then he would give the desk a thorough once-over, his voice trembling with excitement; of course, appraisers get excited by valuable things even when they themselves don't own them. A discovery like this, in a little shop in a nondescript village—anyone would want to get in on that excitement somehow. To have a hand in the discovery.

For the next half hour, Lapin arranged his window, trying to come up with enticing items, not too expensive, that would lure customers into the store. He forgot about Albertine until he heard a scuffling noise in the back and nearly had a heart attack.

"What in the world are you doing, and get away from that desk!" he said, panting as he reached her.

Albertine was on her knees and she got up and brushed her hands on her pants. "Your floor needs sweeping," she said.

It was going to be a long day, thought Lapin, digging deep into himself to find some compassion for this woman he had known all his life, who had never fit in, and who had it so much worse than he did.

"She was struck down by God," said Albertine, pushing past Lapin and going down the aisle.

"Huh?" said Lapin, barely interested.

"You know who," said Albertine.

"Albertine, if you have something to say, just say it. I'm not in a mood for riddles."

Albertine stood staring at the floor and Lapin saw that her hands were quivering. He didn't feel this way often, not before ten in the morning, but what he felt in that moment was a powerful urge for a drink. Something with a good kick—like one of Lawrence's Negronis.

42

1⁹⁹⁶

"Oh, come back to bed, don't worry about that now," he said, his voice like honey.

Cataline Renaud wanted to do as he said. It was not from any resistance to being told what to do that she stayed at the sink, washing dishes, and then began to sweep the floor. It was simply that having a clean and tidy place was a requirement. And nothing—not even desire, not even love—could change that.

He watched as she swept. He watched her get the dustpan from under the sink, cradle the broom with one arm so she could hold the dustpan, and sweep the barely visible dirt into it. He noticed that she did not ask for his help.

"Cataline, Cataline..." he murmured.

She looked up and smiled at him. "Coming," she said.

43

On Wednesday evening, Milo Clavel moved down the main street as though he were a *boulevardier* in *La Belle Époque*. A slightly soiled cravat was tucked into his shirt, and languidly he smoked a Gitane as he walked with his chest out, nodding to passersby. It was chilly and there was no moon, and by the time Milo reached Chez Papa, the boulevardier was hungry and cold.

He pushed the door open, saying a prayer under his breath that he might find a lonely woman inside, preferably with a full wallet.

He breathed in the warm air, redolent of coffee, cigarettes, and frites. Nodded to a friend sitting at the bar. Adjusted the cravat and looked about the room. And there—clouds parting and angels singing—in a booth at the back of the room, sat a woman alone. She was neither old nor young, which he had long felt to be the optimal age. She was neither homely nor pretty—also optimal.

With a grin, Milo slid in across from her. He saw a flash of hope in her eyes before they narrowed. He knew to tread carefully. "It's crowded tonight, do you mind if I share the booth with you?"

She shrugged, looking away.

"Milo Clavel," he said, reaching a hand across the table.

She did not look at him or shake his hand, but she did mumble, "Hortense Depleurisse," just loud enough for him to hear.

"Are you waiting for someone? I can find another seat," he said genially.

Hortense smirked. "I wasn't born yesterday," she said.

"Whyever would you say such a thing? Do you think *I* believe you were born yesterday?" She was more entertaining than he expected. "Because no, far from it. I could tell from the minute I laid eyes on you that you are—"

"Oh, put a cork in it," said Hortense.

"—that you are a woman of parts. Of many

parts. And also that you are a person I would like to know better. Shall we order a little something to eat?"

"You offering to buy?"

"Nothing would give me greater pleasure," Milo said with a smile, feeling in his pocket to see if any euros had magically appeared.

A young woman came by for their orders. Milo copied what Hortense ordered, steak frites, and leaned back in the booth, getting comfortable.

Hortense mumbled something and looked towards the door.

"What's that?" Milo put his hand to his ear and used an old-man voice that he thought hilarious.

Hortense just shook her head slowly, looking at him with what even Milo could tell was contempt.

This is not going well, he thought, drumming his fingers on the table. Am I losing my touch? That Delphine—she doesn't want me ever to get with another woman. She's cursed me from beyond the grave.

Hortense watched Milo's face, saw him get amused by whatever nonsense he was thinking. Delphine was lucky she ate the cheese, she thought, just to get away from this execrable excuse for a man.

SOLANGE MADE her way to the bar at Chez Papa, nodding to various people she had gone to *primaire* with, or dated as a teenager, and then had little to do with since. She waved for Nico's attention and ordered a martini.

"Fancy," said Anne-Marie, whom Solange had squeezed in next to.

"Bonsoir, Anne-Marie," said Solange, her tone formal, as it usually was.

"Bonsoir, Solange. How've you been? You working on a book?"

"I'm always working on a book." She took the drink from Nico and took a long sip, then another.

Anne-Marie watched.

"It's just…I had such hopes," said Lapin on the other side of her. "I thought—and I don't mean just wishful thinking, Anne-Marie, this was different—I thought my ship had finally, at long last, come in. That my endless patience had been wondrously and beautifully rewarded. I just…I just can't believe it, to be honest. It's as though I hear the words that Monsieur Durand said, and of course I know their meaning. But in some enormous way, I do *not* understand, I do not comprehend."

Anne-Marie had heard a version of this approximately 87,000 times since that morning when he had called to tell her what the appraiser had said. She patted his arm, still watching Solange out of the corner of her eye.

"What's the book about?" she asked her.

Solange looked at Anne-Marie, puzzled. "Which book?"

"The book you just said you are writing."

"Oh!" Solange took a long pull on the martini. She wiped her mouth in a manly, dockworker sort of way. "It's about Deconstructionism. It's boring as all hell."

Anne-Marie's eyebrows went up. She had no idea what to say to that so she said nothing.

"It's only that—the degree of skill, it's practically unimaginable. Superhuman. *Celestial*," said Lapin. For the 87,001 time. "Even Monsieur Durand said I was not to feel embarrassed about being duped, that nearly anyone would have drawn the same conclusion. Let me ask you this: did you have any idea that there were such skilled forgers among us?"

"Among us? Do you mean in Castillac?"

"No," said Lapin irritably. "I mean in this insane, duplicitous world we live in."

"Well, I suppose if you're going to be a forger, you have to be very good at it or you won't get anywhere at all. I mean, you can be a second-rate or a third or even a fourth-rate furniture maker, and all that will happen is you don't get to charge as much."

"Your logic is not soothing to my spirit."

Anne-Marie thought of a few things to say but smiled at Lapin and kept her mouth shut.

44

On the outskirts of Castillac, when night fell, it fell hard. It was so dark one couldn't see the shapes of trees or bushes or barns, only dense blackness. It was cold and the night was quiet, with no sound of birds or bugs or any creatures stirring, including mice.

The Renaud farmhouse had no lights on and its inhabitants were sound asleep.

It was child's play to get in through the locked kitchen door—Madame Renaud's stinginess had allowed for only the cheapest lock to be installed, which required no skill and almost no dexterity to pop open with a simple screwdriver.

Ironic, he thought, that she spent the money and it was wasted. Most of Castillac left their doors open all the time, even when they were not home.

He crept into the kitchen and inhaled, smelling a dish with considerable rosemary. Considered opening the refrigerator to see if there was any left over. But then decided to do the job he had come to do, and get it over with.

As he crept down the hallway, a floorboard creaked; he stood with one foot in the air, holding his breath.

No sound except for a light snore, rather dainty, that told him which room she was in.

The door was cracked open and he gently pushed it. It too creaked, he winced, and Madame Renaud sat up in bed.

There was not a moment to be lost.

He lunged on top of her and put his hands around her throat.

Her thoughts coming in milliseconds, Madame Renaud almost called for Gilbert but stopped herself.

A gurgle came from deep inside as he squeezed harder.

With one hand she reached to the drawer of the bedside table and felt for the box cutter. She grabbed it, and stabbed him in the ribs with all her might and fury, and then slashed across his back.

He cursed her, amazed, then in shock. He sat

up and reached around, felt the slippery wetness of his own bleeding.

"Get out," rasped Madame Renaud, who had leapt out of bed and was brandishing the box cutter.

After the smallest possible pause, that is what he did.

IV

45

Chief Charlot was groggy, having been awakened from a deep sleep, but her uniform and hair were in order even if her mind was still catching up. Cataline Renaud had called just after midnight and insisted on meeting her at the gendarmerie.

"Please, I ask you to go over the events again," the Chief said, rubbing her temples. "You were asleep in bed. And then?"

"I've already told you," said Madame Renaud, her voice still raspy. She stood up, agitated, stroking her neck. "He broke in—through the kitchen door—and then jumped on my bed and tried to strangle me. It's a miracle I'm alive!"

At this, Gilbert, whom she had not wanted to

leave at home alone for obvious reasons, looked up. His face was hard to read.

"What did the assailant look like?"

"It was pitch dark. I didn't see him at all."

"It wasn't someone you know?"

"No."

"You're certain? You know of no one who wishes you harm?"

"What are you getting at?" said Madame Renaud. "What are you implying?" She shrank back, glaring. Charlot thought she could see her shoulders trembling slightly.

"Only asking standard questions, please calm yourself. Did you notice any identifying marks—tattoos, moles, or the like?"

"I said it was pitch dark."

"This sort of thing doesn't happen around here," said the Chief, leaning back in her chair.

"Apparently it does," said Madame Renaud, even more agitated. "But I was prepared. I kept that box cutter beside my bed precisely because a single mother can't be too careful."

"Did you have an expectation that someone might attack you? How long had you kept the box-cutter there?"

"You're making it sound as though I did something wrong. I am the victim, not the perpetrator!"

Charlot rubbed her eyes. "Do you think the

wounds you inflicted were superficial? Will he need a doctor, a hospital?"

"I keep telling you: it was pitch dark. I have no idea. I stabbed him with all my might, I can tell you that much," Madame Renaud said, unable to hide a small smile. She mumbled something.

"What?" asked the Chief.

"Nothing. I was just—I was cursing him. Not language I wish to repeat."

Charlot pulled her elbows off her desk and considered next steps.

"What do you propose to do to ensure my safety and the safety of my boy? If there's a strangler roaming Castillac, tell me: what's to be done? Where should we go? How are we going to stay safe?"

There was a sort of distance—and hopelessness—in her voice that Chief Charlot heard and noted. It almost sounded as though Madame Renaud were reading from a script.

"We will follow the usual procedures," the Chief said, reaching out to touch the other woman on the arm. She could feel the tension in Madame Renaud's body. "Right now, you need to see a doctor. There's bruising on your neck and you should be checked out to make sure you're all right."

Madame Renaud waved her hand. "I don't need a doctor. I'm fine. But I will most assuredly *not* be fine about going to sleep in my house tonight knowing that man is still at large. I was thinking… maybe you could post Paul-Henri at my house for the time being? She said this in a small, supplicating voice, unusual for her. Again, Gilbert looked at his mother, his expression inscrutable.

"The doctor is necessary to document what has happened," the Chief said. "Did you hear any car or motorcycle after he left? Did you go to the window to see which direction he went?"

"I went straight to Gilbert's room to see if he was all right," said Madame Renaud, and at that memory—of the fear that the man had done something to the boy before coming to her room—she broke down.

She had not wept in public since she was a child. She was, altogether, not a weeper in private either. Gilbert's eyes were wide as he watched his mother, and he felt such a mixture of emotions that finally he closed his eyes to try to think of something else.

46

Ben was laughing so hard he had to bend over and put his hands on his knees.

"Well...I wasn't trying to be funny," said Molly.

"I know!" He laughed again, shaking his head. "It's just—any French person would know, but of course there's no reason you would."

"Does it have something to do with birth records? Because really, I never dreamed a visit to the mairie could be so hilarious."

"No no—it's that 'Jean Moulin' is not some random *mec* who lives around here—he's a famous —maybe *the most* famous—Resistance leader from World War II. He was from farther south, not from the Dordogne, so maybe that's why you didn't recognize the name. Have you noticed in a lot of French villages there is rue Jean Moulin, or Place Jean Moulin, or Pont Jean Moulin? He's quite a beloved figure."

"Well, now that you mention it, the name did ring a bell," she said, starting to snicker. "So tell me this—was Madame Renaud making a joke when she filled out the form, or is the name so common it actually could be the name of Gilbert's father, as well as the Resistance leader's?"

Ben shrugged. "Of course I can't say for sure. But if I were placing a bet? I'd bet on Madame Renaud wanting to keep the parentage a secret, and sort of thumbing her nose at the father, in a bureaucratic way, by making it a joke. It's quite French, actually."

Molly nodded, chewing her lip. "And so…the obvious question is: why did she want to keep this secret? Was he married? Someone famous or notorious for some reason, maybe a criminal?"

"Someone who simply did not want her to have the child?"

"Someone who was threatening her to keep his name out of it? Or was she the one who did not want him involved?"

"Any or all of the above?"

Molly heaved a sigh. "Looks like I've got my work cut out for me on this one. I so hoped it would be an easy little job and I could quickly put

Gilbert's mind at rest. Now it feels like I've stepped into…what? Some kind of mess I don't understand. As for Madame Renaud—my impression of her was so…I thought she was a stick-in-the-mud who worked too hard, was too strict with her boy, and maybe a little paranoid about the dangers of the world. Now it turns out she had an illicit relationship with someone who—"

"Well, we don't know. It might simply be the usual story, she got knocked up and the guy didn't want to marry her, and she left his name off the form out of spite."

"Mm," said Molly. "Maybe." But somehow…she felt the story was more complicated than that. Who would know? Who could she ask without alerting Madame Renaud that she was sniffing around subjects that were one hundred percent none of her business?

༄

"You got any plans this weekend?" Frances asked. "My plans involve poop, pretty much all day long," she added. Baby Luka continued to have some digestive problems.

"Nothing," said Molly. "Changeover Day tomorrow, of course, but no dinner parties or anything else going on that I know of. It's not winter yet, but people seem to be hunkering down already, warming their feet by the fire."

"Do you ever think—just for a second—what in the world are we doing in this little backwater village in the middle of nowhere?"

Before Molly could answer, her phone buzzed and she pulled it out to see a text from Ben.

Molly cocked her head and looked out the window.

"Yes?"

Molly chewed on her lip, which was starting to bleed by this point.

"Molly!"

"Madame Renaud was attacked last night, at home. She's okay. But someone tried to strangle her."

"Madame Renaud? That old sourpuss?"

"The very same."

"I mean, she's not a delight to be around, but why would anyone want to kill her?"

"Who knows if she was the specific target."

"So just like that, you're saying we have random stranglers roaming this backwater village now, and he just happened to stumble into her house?"

"Maybe. We have no idea."

"Molly! Listen to me now. You can't be sitting there thinking all you have to do is lie around and feel smug about your pregnancy—get out on the streets and investigate, sister! I don't like the sound of this at all!"

Molly was looking down at the floor, now sort of maniacally scraping a bit of skin off her lower lip with her teeth.

"What," said Frances.

"It's just...something," murmured Molly.

Luka let out a sudden squall and Frances jumped up to go to her.

"Not to sound like a know-it-all, since as you well know I'm no expert on babies—but something you can't yet understand: once you're a mother? Once that baby is placed in your arms? You realize you will die if anything happens to your child," said Frances. "I mean, not exaggerating: *die*."

"It's a little strange hearing that come out of your mouth."

"Well, the whole enterprise is still a little strange, and I expect that's going to continue until our children are grown and we're on the porch in our rockers. But listen," said Frances with vehemence, while taking a peek to see if Luka needing changing. "I bring this up because the idea of a violent person on the loose, in our village...I can't bear it. You've gotta get out on the street and find out what's going on, get that guy arrested. We've got babies—and babies-to-be—to protect! Get going, Molls!"

Molly nodded and left. She wasn't used to seeing Frances anxious, even scared. But she did understand: first there were people dropping dead every five minutes, and once that was figured out, now we've got a strangler. It wasn't easy to manage in your mind, mother or no.

All I ever wanted was some peace and quiet with maybe a few almond croissants, thought Molly.

That small complaint out of the way, she was already making a mental list of who she should talk to, with Madame Renaud right at the top.

47

The next morning, Molly left the Saturday cleaning to Constance and went early to the market. She had three balls in the air: who was Gilbert's father? Who attacked Madame Renaud? And—because Molly was nothing if not dogged—did Delphine really eat the cheese?

She wondered if Madame Renaud was all right and if she would be lucky enough to see her at the market. Not for the first time, Molly wished she had a good relationship with the doctors in town. And by "good relationship," she meant "would blab to me about the personal business of his patients."

Manette was in her sights when someone familiar yet unexpected caught her eye.

"Well—I—holy Moses! Bonjour!" said Molly, eyes wide. "I'm so surprised to see you!"

"Bonjour to you," said Selma Throckmorton, beaming, then rubbing her belly. She looked to be about six months along.

"My heavens, congratulations!" Molly added. Desperately she wanted to ask if it was Florian's baby—she barely stopped the words from tumbling out of her mouth in a rush. Instead, she stood with her mouth open, groping for something else to say and finding nothing.

"And congratulations are clearly in order for you too," said Selma, grinning. "Is it something in the Castillac water?" she said, and tilted her head back and laughed, so loud that market-goers turned to look.

Molly was still gaping. She wanted to ask: does Florian know you're here? Was he expecting you?

Is that baby his??

Finally she let out a sort of croak but Selma had moved on, enjoying the congratulations of various strangers, and Molly could hear that braying laugh off and on for the rest of the time she was at the market.

Molly rubbed a hand over her face and tried to collect herself.

Babies, she thought. So commonplace, yet so mysterious. And oh the trouble they can cause.

Manette was thankfully, for the moment, without customers, and Molly headed straight to her. They said their bonjours and kissed cheeks.

"Terrible about Madame Renaud."

Molly nodded. They stood for a moment in silence.

"Ha," said Manette.

"What do you mean ha?"

"I've known you for years now. And I can see you've got a list of questions. So come on, ask away."

Molly didn't love seeming so transparent but shrugged that off. She leaned in to whisper. "Well, first of all...do you think that's Florian's baby?"

Manette laughed. "Who knows? But it would be a little strange—and cruel—if it isn't, wouldn't you say? Why come back here otherwise?"

"Yes. Though people can be cruel, of course. It's not exactly a rarity."

Manette shrugged and neatened up a pile of squash. "What else you got?"

"Just this, really: you were friends with Delphine."

Manette nodded.

"And I'm trying to work out if she...if she also died because of Lela's cheese. I'm probably being overly cautious. But I'm wondering if you saw her during the few days before she died, and if you did, was Lela's cheese involved? Just between us, Charlot says there was. But I'd like some verification."

"You don't trust Charlot?"

"Oh, sure, I trust her. I mean, I don't think she's lying about it. But that doesn't mean her information is correct."

Manette nodded.

There was something, Molly thought. She could see it on Manette's face, which was usually warm and smiling but now looked hesitant, possibly even troubled.

"I didn't see her. Not on Sunday, anyway. I don't leave the farm on Sundays, as a rule."

"How about Monday?"

Manette shrugged again. "You're talking awhile ago, now—but no, not that Monday, pretty sure I'd have remembered since it would have been the last time I saw her alive."

Suddenly Molly's eyes got every wide. She reached out and grasped Manette's arm and squeezed it. "Oh! Honestly, I think this baby is turning my brain into pudding!"

Manette nodded. "Yes, that's part of the deal."

"*I* saw Delphine the day before she died. In Chez Papa. I even spoke to her. I can't believe I completely forgot!"

Manette started to say something but Molly

rushed off, waving over her shoulder, without even making a quick trip to Patisserie Bujold, on her way to the Renaud farm.

※

BUT AT THE FARM, no one was home. Molly walked to the barn, hoping Gilbert might be hanging around, but he and Madame Renaud were nowhere to be seen.

Which made sense, she realized: would they feel safe here even in daylight, with the attacker still on the loose?

Are *any* of us safe here? she wondered.

She drove the scooter back into the village, this time heading for Patisserie Bujold, so distracted by her thoughts that she drove uncharacteristically slowly.

She wandered into the shop. It's so puzzling, she thought. As though the literal pieces of two separate jigsaw puzzles have been mixed together, and somehow we have to separate them.

Quickly she scanned Edmond's customers and saw Solange standing in line.

"Bonjour, Solange," said Molly. "We barely know each other, but I wonder if you would have a coffee with me?"

Solange looked pained. She wanted to say no,

Molly could see that, but after a pause the woman nodded and summoned up a weak smile.

They got their espressos and croissants and sat at one of the little inside cafe tables. Molly noticed a couple of people in line giving them looks, but she had no idea what to make of that or if there was anything to make of it. People are curious, that's all, she thought.

"Are you going to interrogate me?" Solange asked, trying to play it as a joke.

"What?" Molly was taken aback. The truth was, of course, that that was exactly what she wanted to do.

She laughed, trying to put the other woman at ease. "No bright lights and torture techniques," she said, grinning. "But if you're amenable, I do have a question or two. Do you mind?" Solange was looking at her lap.

Molly continued. "It's only that I want to put the whole goat cheese case to rest, you understand? Such a terrible chapter in Castillac history! And of course, I feel terrible for poor Lela, and hope her business recovers quickly. Her cheese is a marvel, a treasure. I'm looking forward to the day she returns to the market with a full inventory."

Solange nodded, waiting.

"Thing is, I could use your help with this one… this one unresolved question," Molly said. She lowered her voice to barely audible, "which is this: do we one hundred percent know, without any doubt, that Delphine ate Lela's cheese? Did anyone actually see this take place? Because if I can find a witness, someone to confirm seeing that happen, then —of course with great sorrow for all the victims of this chance, weird, unfortunate occurrence—we can call it case closed and move on."

Molly paused, watching Solange's face.

"And if you can't?" Solange whispered. "Then what?"

Molly made an expression that meant: you can guess. And it's not good.

"She was murdered," Solange said, so quietly that Molly had to read her lips.

Molly nodded. "It wouldn't for certain mean murder. But it would definitely need looking into."

Solange looked at the door as though wishing she could fly right through it and away from Molly. She sighed and wrapped her arms around herself. She took a sip of her espresso and looked at the croissant on the plate but made no move to pick it up.

Molly knew to be patient even when she didn't want to be.

Finally Solange said quietly, "If I tell you something, do you swear never to say it came from me?"

Molly nodded, barely daring to hope.

"No, I mean it, don't just nod, I want you to swear!"

"I swear," said Molly.

"It's not as though I'm the only person who knows this. We all grew up together," said Solange.

Molly was holding her breath, no idea what the other woman was about to say.

"Delphine…" said Solange. She looked again at the door as though someone might come through it and save her from having to finish. "Obviously… this is rather unusual in France, land of a million cheeses. But Delphine was…she was lactose intolerant. She never, ever ate cheese. It made her…not fit for human company, if you understand me."

Molly's mind was racing all over the place. "I think I do," she said. She stared at a piece of scrap paper on the floor while her mind frantically tried to fit the puzzle pieces together. "Please don't think me terribly rude—but I need to get somewhere," she said, standing up and shoving the rest of her croissant in her mouth and washing it down with the rest of her espresso. "You've been hugely, hugely helpful. Thank you. I won't say a word about where I got this information," she said, and was gone.

Edmond had been watching this meeting out of the corner of his eye and he was dreadfully curious about why Molly had jumped up so suddenly and raced off.

Had Solange insulted her? Did it have anything to do with what his customers were now calling The Castillac Strangler?

48

1977

THE GIRLS WERE STANDING outside the cantine, just before the afternoon classes were due to begin. "Well, is it any surprise, really? Haven't we always thought he was horrible and undeserving of her?" said Solange.

Manette shook her head slowly. Always one for giving people benefit of the doubt, she was trying to find a loophole, a reason, an explanation, for why a person would—

"I want to hurt him," said Solange.

Marielle looked nervous.

"It's not really our business," said Manette.

"Not our business? This is Delphine we're talking about. One for all and all for one," said Solange. "If some cretin did that to you, would you want us to sit back and say it was none of our business? Or would you want us to take action? Decisive action," she added, with a dark expression.

Marielle and Manette stared at the ground.

Tears fell down Manette's cheeks but she did not move to wipe them away. Marielle was rubbing her arms and making quiet grunting noises.

Albertine was around the corner of the building and she edged up closer to hear what the other girls were talking about.

"Well?" said Solange. "Quickly now, class is starting in a few minutes. Let's have some ideas. If it were only me, I'd want to meet him in a dark alley with a tire iron. But I understand that's not everyone's style. I'm open to other suggestions. But we cannot let him get away with this."

"The thing is," whispered Manette, "if we hurt him in some way, especially in public, he's going to turn around and make things even worse for Delphine. Anything we do, he's going to do worse to her, times a thousand."

Solange was not a person who was used to being wrong or who tolerated it easily. But to her credit, she realized Manette was correct and acknowledged it.

"Then what," she said, her eyes for once welling up as well. "Then we're doomed to silence, and doing nothing but watching our friend—"

"Yes," said Manette. "Awful as that is."

"For now, we wait," said Marielle. "But who knows. I'm not really one for prayer but I will be praying for this: that one day a moment appears when we can make this right. Or at least—we can make him suffer."

Solange shot Marielle a look of gratitude. She was glad not to be the only one among them who had a thirst for vengeance.

49

Malcolm Barstow woke on Sunday with the sun in his face and his back sore. He swung his feet to the floor and sat for a moment with his head in his hands.

"You look like it was your mother who died," said Daisy, who was standing in the kitchen with a cup of espresso and a smirk on her face.

"This sofa is like a torture device," he said, standing and stretching.

"You could have slept in my mother's bed."

Malcolm walked to Daisy and put his hands on her shoulders. "Why do you say things like that?" he asked, and it was a genuine question. "I'm only trying to help you."

"Maybe I don't want any help."

"I don't believe you. I think you don't feel like you deserve help. Or, you think somebody's gonna want payback."

She turned away, not wanting him to see her face. "Now you're my therapist?"

"You're not hard to read."

"Mm." She busied herself with the espresso machine and didn't look at him.

The machine did its business, hissing and sputtering, and Daisy handed Malcolm the cup with a lovely crema on top.

"Thanks," he said, grinning at her. "So okay, I'm going to jump right in. Like—what in the world are you gonna do with your life, how are you going to take care of the basic stuff?"

Daisy looked up at the ceiling and Malcolm thought he had made her cry. Then she raked her hands through her hair and swallowed hard.

"I killed her," she said quietly.

"You really shouldn't go around saying that," said Malcolm. "Even though it was those ridiculous goats that killed everybody. But still."

Daisy squinted at him, stood very still for a moment, then shrugged. "I mean, I know I didn't stab her or anything like that, but I was so awful I might as well have. This whole time we've been here, in Castillac, I was spewing a stream of criticism, all the time. Nothing but complaining. I didn't want to come here. Castillac was stupid. She was stupid. My father was stupid. I wasn't even clever with my insults, just relentless. Of course I didn't want to come here! All my friends are in New York! And I blamed her…I blamed her for everything."

She turned away and sipped her espresso. Malcolm nodded but did not try to change her mind.

"And now I blame her for dying," said Daisy, and then after a moment, she started to laugh.

Malcolm joined in. They laughed so hard their stomach muscles were sore later. And after a few minutes of hilarity, Daisy started to shake with sobs, uncontrollably, the grief finally making its way to the surface.

50

First thing in the morning, Molly took the scooter to the épicerie. Marielle was at the register, ringing up a small random collection of things for a young man. Molly wandered just a few steps down an aisle, eavesdropping of course, but Marielle and the customer only spoke about the weather and the price of laundry detergent. Molly was trying to figure out what tack to take with Marielle: tricky, because she didn't know what she didn't know, and the wrong question could cause her to clam up.

All Molly knew was that Delphine's friends were acting squirrelly.

Delphine hadn't eaten the cheese. That was a fact. The goats and the crocus had not killed her.

Florian had determined Delphine died from a heart attack, which from investigative experience, Molly knew could be caused by many things. She wondered if Florian had done a tox screen on all the victims—that was standard, right?

For a moment, pretending to look at packages of noodles, Molly considered motive. Delphine had no assets as far as Molly knew, and Molly doubted she was murdered by a competitor for the attentions of the odious Milo Clavell. So what was left for motive? Was it possible that some old resentment or hurt had been her undoing, something going all the way back to school days?

Was that why her friends were so jumpy, so resistant to making eye contact, so…guilty-looking?

"Can I help you?" asked Marielle, and Molly startled, then walked back towards the register.

"Hi, Marielle, how are you this morning?"

"Dandy," Marielle answered, with sarcasm. "And by the way, I know you know."

"I know?"

"About the cheese. And Delphine."

So the women were in close touch. Interesting.

"It's curious, isn't it? What do you think?"

Marielle scowled. "What I think is that there are too many people in this village willing to do horrible things. Maybe it's all of humanity, I don't know. It's always been this way, it's nothing new, and I'm sick of it. Sick of worrying, sick of listening for the next shoe to drop. Delphine actually managed to escape this place, and then managed to get sucked back in, and now look."

"Do you think she was murdered?" Molly said quietly.

Marielle opened her mouth but at the same moment Madame Tessier came into the shop and Marielle and Molly greeted her.

"I heard about the cheese," said Madame Tessier, looking pointedly at Molly.

"I guess the secret is no longer a secret," said Molly.

"Who's been blabbing?" said Marielle, looking pointedly at Molly.

"Why are you both staring at me like that?"

"The village—yet again—is very unsettled," said Madame Tessier. "I don't have to spell it out for you, Molly—if Delphine wasn't killed by the cheese, then what—or who—killed her?"

"It's entirely possible, Madame Tessier—no, make that probable—that she simply died of a heart attack, like people do. Just as Florian said. It's hardly an unusual, exotic occurrence."

"She was only in her early fifties."

Molly shrugged. "All right then, you both believe she was murdered? Why do you think that? Do you know something? Do you have someone in mind who is capable and motivated to do such a thing?"

Marielle was grimacing but she bent her head down so Molly couldn't see her expression. She shook her head slowly but did not answer.

"I've got nothing," said Madame Tessier, though it pained her very much to admit it.

❧

MOLLY MADE her way to the coroner's office. Florian was not there.

"Bonjour, Matthias."

"Bonjour, Molly, what can I do for you?" He glanced back at his computer and Molly understood that she was disturbing his work.

"If you've got half a second, I've got a general question about the autopsy process. Is it routine—if you know—to do tox screens on all deaths?"

"Well, that's not a simple question to answer."

"Educate me."

Matthias sighed and looked at the door. For once, he wished Florian would arrive, so he could pass Molly over to him. He liked Molly; he appreciated her efforts at justice. But all he wanted to do that morning was get through a list of tasks on his computer, not get dragged down any rabbit holes. Molly was, God love her, the queen of rabbit holes.

"Well, not all autopsies are the same. Their goals are not the same. And when the goal is different, the process is different."

"Huh?"

"If there is suspicion of foul play, the autopsy is more complete, as you'd imagine. Or if a drug overdose is suspected, then the tox screen would be more involved and covering the bases of likely drugs. If all you're looking for is confirming the cause of death, where there is no particular complication or suspicion—then the process is fairly simple, and only a handful of things will be tested for."

Molly was nodding, drinking all of this in. "So you're saying there are different levels of tox screens?"

"Oh my yes! We wouldn't want to test everything on everyone—it would cost a fortune and take forever. So we choose what seems appropriate based on the circumstances."

"And...these recent deaths...?"

Just then Florian burst through the door. He was standing up straight, his chest out, a bright smile on his face. Not a smile—a grin. The likes of which Molly had never before seen on the coroner's face.

Molly beamed at him. Then, without saying a word, she went over and shook his hand and then hugged him. Congratulations," she murmured, and she felt his body tremble a little, still in shock, but tremendously, insanely, unexpectedly happy.

※

As Molly was leaving the village, she spotted Gilbert playing basketball with another boy in the small park on the edge of town. Gilbert sightings were rare enough that she figured she should talk to him, even though she didn't exactly have news.

"First of all, I'm so sorry about what happened! You and you mother must have been terrified."

Gilbert made a sort of face and Molly realized too late that she had insulted his incipient manhood.

"I mean, everyone in the world would be terrified if a strange person broke in and tried to strangle somebody, much less your mother!"

"I slept through it," Gilbert said, looking at the ground. "I didn't do anything."

"I bet your mother is tremendously glad about that," Molly said.

Gilbert sighed.

"So...what's happening with that situation?" asked Molly. "Is Chief Charlot telling you anything about the investigation? Oh—you know what?—would you and your mother like to come stay at La

Baraque? Just to have some more people around and a dog who's not exactly a fierce guard but at least she's noisy? I hate thinking of the two of you at the farm, worrying about your safety. Not that I think your mother is a target, it was probably just random that it was your house—" Molly realized she was talking too much.

"Thanks, Molly. I wish we were at La Baraque. But we're staying with a friend of my mother's, Madame Severin?"

Molly nodded. "I know her, a little bit." She thought about a case from a few years back. Lucie Severin was not a happy woman, and she had had good reasons for her unhappiness.

Gilbert kicked a rock. "Any luck on my case?"

Molly took a deep breath. "Well, I thought I'd cracked it for about five minutes. I did find your birth record. But the paternal name was made up, I'm afraid."

Gilbert shrugged and Molly wanted to hug him.

"You know how it is, investigations take patience," she said. "I'll get there eventually. Get back to your game, I'll find you if I find out anything. And stay safe—"

She watched the boy as he rejoined his game, and then suddenly turned back to the center of the village.

Sometimes Molly felt an urge to do something though she could think of no justification for doing it.

She tended to follow those urges.

Which was how she ended up knocking on Lucie Severin's door, with no questions in mind, only the sense that she needed to be there for reasons that would hopefully become apparent at some point.

Lucie opened the door just a crack, and then halfway once she saw it was Molly.

"Bonjour, Madame Sutton," she said.

Chilly.

"Bonjour, Madame Severin," said Molly. "Excuse me for bothering you. I wonder if I might come in for a moment?"

51

Paul-Henri sat on the edge of his chair, pretending to work on some files but keeping a close eye on his boss. Chantal was jumpy. Paul-Henri steeled himself for her unpleasant mood, one way or another, to turn on him.

Chantal was absorbed with whatever was on her computer screen. She raked her fingers through her hair, half undoing her tight bun. She tapped one foot. She cleared her throat and stared at Paul-Henri.

"What are you doing, pawing through those files as though they have any importance whatsoever?" she blurted out.

Though Paul-Henri had been waiting for it, he startled anyway.

"We have a strangler to catch," she growled. "Get on the street. Find him." She paused. "Pay Milo Clavel a visit, will you? And don't be too polite with him. He's not going to respond to that. You're going to have to frighten him a little."

"Do you think Milo—and Madame Renaud?"

Chantal looked up from her computer with a stony glare.

One of Paul-Henri's talents was older women and how to handle them, including the Chief, and he didn't even consider asking any more questions, but quickly stood, patted his uniform, and was out the door.

52

"That was some excellent work, Molly," Ben said, at the kitchen table chopping onions with a prodigiously sharp knife.

"Of course I'm pleased, and grateful to Lucie. But...it's complicated, isn't it? Is this a case where possibly it would be prudent to let sleeping dogs lie?"

"You mean don't tell Gilbert?"

"Yes. I mean—of course I hate the idea of not telling him. Of knowing and keeping it to myself. That's just not right. But..."

"Madame Renaud will despise you forever."

"And she'd have a right to. I was not interfering to solve any crime, just poking my nose in where it doesn't belong. And it's not only that.

The longer I live here, the more the village of Castillac, while sturdy and resilient in a lot of ways, also maintains...how to say this...there's something of a delicate balance, necessary because of the lifelong histories you all have with each other. A balance between knowing other people's business and letting them alone about it."

"Of course we pride ourselves in knowing all that business in every gory, salacious detail."

Molly laughed. "Oh, I realize, believe me. When we finally told people about the baby, I saw a few people scurry out of Chez Papa and I swear they were heading out to be first to spread the news. Of course that's harmless, nothing wrong with that. But when the news isn't good, when it's complicated, when there are sides to choose...."

"Whole different thing."

"Yes. And sometimes...I notice people putting on blinders. Because without them? Living here would be just too much. No privacy at all. So people sort of pretend there are curtains here and there, if you see what I mean, blocking out the past, so we're not consumed by it."

Ben nodded. "That is a good way of describing it. Some people do let the past stay in the past. But others—some people never forget anything. If you insulted their best friend all the way back in primaire, they're going to remember and hold it against you."

Molly watched him chop, absorbed by the growing pile of diced onion and the smell of garlic, already minced. "Well, the week began with three questions to answer, and I've only one accomplished, and the easiest by far. Still nothing on who had means, motive, or opportunity to kill Delphine. Or even any certainty that she was killed. And who attacked Madame Renaud? Could Delphine's killer—if there is one—and Renaud's attacker be the same person? Why? And I still have no idea what is up with Delphine's old friends. They're hiding something, I have no doubt of that. But is it important? Does it have anything to do with Delphine's death, or does it belong behind one of the curtains because it has no bearing on anything in the present?"

Ben put the knife down and looked at Molly. "You'll get there," he said. He was quite happy to see Molly back to her old cogitating self.

THE NEXT MORNING, Molly guiltily put off Frances who was in desperate need of "adult contact," as she put it, in order to pay a visit to Manette at her farm.

She had questions, but most of them were difficult to put into words, because pretty much all she had was suspicion attached to no specific persons. In other words: feelings, not evidence. Not a place any investigator wants to be.

"Well bonjour, Molly!" said Manette when she answered the door. Her usually open and warm expression had a sort of veil over it once again, Molly thought.

"You're not happy to see me," said Molly.

"Oh! It's not that," said Manette, but offered no explanation.

"I've come to interrogate you," said Molly with a big smile, hoping to break through with a joke.

"I don't much like the sound of that."

"Manette. It's me, Molly! You know I have nothing but affection for you. And for the village and everyone in it. I'm only...it's that...there's something...something is unresolved. And you know I just can't let that alone, I need to get to the bottom of whatever it is. I know it, I can smell it! And I believe you are currently my best bet for helping me work out what has happened. You and Delphine were very tight back in the day, correct? Along with the rest of your gang—Marielle, Solange...am I leaving anyone out?"

"We were the four musketeers," said Manette, looking down at the floor. "I was a few years younger, and proud to be included. But all of that was a long time ago." She stepped to the side to let Molly in, closed the door, and leaned against it. "It's, well...you understand I always want to be helpful to you, Molly. You know I trust you. But sometimes...sometimes digging up the past isn't exactly in the best interests of the present. Surely you can see that?"

Molly nodded. "Of course. But if your friend was murdered..."

Manette looked at Molly, her eyes wide. With surprise, or fear? Molly wasn't sure.

A girl wandered into the room banging on a toy drum and singing nonsense.

"Émilie, did you pick up those toys in your room?"

Émilie stopped, fixed her mother with a stare, and kept banging the drum. Manette held eye contact with a neutral expression and said nothing more. Émilie sighed and turned back, still banging, but with less fervor.

When the girl was gone, Manette said quietly, "Is that really what you think? She was murdered?"

"I wish I knew for sure. But this is the situation: as you know, six villagers died as a result of eating poisoned cheese. We know Delphine did not eat the cheese. So maybe she died of a heart attack and there's nothing to see here but the tragedy of a woman whose life ended too soon."

Molly gave Manette some time to think this over.

"Or maybe," continued Molly, "someone took the opportunity of those other deaths, coming fast and furious, dazzling the village with grief and panic, to try to hide Delphine's death among them. That killer—if there *is* a killer—wouldn't have had any idea how the other six died. Maybe he—or she—guessed a serial killer was at work. Who knows? He—or she—wouldn't be able to predict that Delphine's lactose intolerance would separate her from the others and allow us to focus on her cause of death. Because we know that cause was not the same as the rest."

"Sneaky bastard."

Molly cocked her head. "A man, then, you think?"

Manette turned pale, Molly thought.

"Isn't it usually?" asked Manette, a little too loudly.

"Yes. But not always. And so we must leave that question open until we have evidence that closes it."

Manette shrugged and turned away.

"What I came to ask about," said Molly, in as soft and inviting a voice as she could muster, "is whether some event in the past might have bearing on the present situation. Perhaps from quite a long time ago? Might there be some old grievance, a betrayal, the kind of thing that is hard to put to rest...did Delphine hurt someone badly, and that person never forgot it, and decided—perhaps impulsively—to take the chance for revenge?"

Manette was shaking her head. She looked up at the low farmhouse ceiling, then reached up and touched one of the beams with her fingertips. "Don't we all have pasts filled with good moments and bad? Don't we all have memories of...of times when we were unhappy, or hurt, or had a...a situation that was really difficult? Isn't this simply part of life?"

Molly nodded. She let a long moment pass before adding, "The thing is, some people make peace with that, and others...do not." She looked out of the window at the rolling meadow. "Let me ask you an uncomfortable question," said Molly. "First of all, thanks for letting me interrupt your day, I know you have a million things to do. And I know this is unwelcome territory, but here goes: you are one musketeer, and Delphine was another. Do you have any reason—any at all—to think that any of the other musketeers has been nursing a dangerous resentment all this time?"

Manette sighed. She looked Molly forthrightly in the eyes and said, "No."

Molly waited to see if she was going to add anything else, but Manette did not. She jumped up. Molly thought she looked flustered.

"Would you like a coffee?" asked Manette. "Excuse my manners."

Molly nodded enthusiastically. "Not at all. Will I get some of Delilah's cream?

"Absolutely." Manette bustled about in the kitchen and Molly drifted into the sitting room. A knitting basket sat next to an armchair that had a bit of stuffing poking from the side. The woodstove wasn't lit but the room was still cozy and familial. A toy flute was on the rug along with a red marker. She heard the piping voices of children quarreling down a hallway.

For a moment Molly lost all thought of murder and Delphine Bardot and imagined La Baraque in a year's time, and how the sitting room might have children's books scattered about, and a rattle, and who knows what else. Even the smell of the room would be different—

"Molly? You look a million miles away." Manette handed her a mug.

"Thanks. Just having a little daydream about the baby. Sometimes I find it hard to focus on anything else, you know?"

Manette smiled. "Oh yes. Are you planning to keep working, after the baby comes?"

Molly laughed. "I expect so. Have to put food on the table, right? Hopefully the gîte business rebounds before long."

They drank their coffee.

"Babies," said Molly, shaking her head.

"I know."

"Is my life going to be completely, I don't know, unrecognizable?"

"Yes." Manette laughed. "But in the best sort of way. A baby who's wanted brings joy, and that's all you need to know." She sat on the edge of her chair, patting her knees nervously. A long moment passed. Molly waited, could feel the pressure of what Manette both wanted and didn't want to say.

"And then...a baby who is not wanted, that is something else altogether," Manette said, so quietly that Molly had to strain to hear the words.

"Tell me," said Molly.

Manette's eyes filled with tears. "Help me, God," she said, crossing herself. "I have kept this secret for so long, I never thought—"

53

"I've never seen you like this."

"Surely you have."

"I have not. Your cheeks are rosy, your eyes wet—"

"This is the effect you have on me. Selma—"

She grinned, and her mouth was so wide the grin was almost literally ear-to-ear. Her lipstick was smeared and her hair tousled.

"Yes?" she whispered. "What effect, exactly?"

"Marry me."

Selma pulled back, put her hands on Florian's shoulders, and looked at him closely. "You've never said those words before, have you?"

"Of course not. You—"

"Hold on. Do you feel...forced into it? Because

of...my condition?" She reached down and rubbed her belly.

"Where have you gotten the idea that I would allow myself to be forced to do anything?"

"Not how you roll," she said, grinning.

"No." He waited. He had asked a question and she had bobbed and weaved and not answered it. Why oh why, thought Florian, did women torment him so?

54

On Wednesday, after a poor night's sleep followed by a huge breakfast, Molly had a second cup of coffee (with cream) and stared out the window, trying to focus her attention on the unanswered questions about Delphine's death.

"I used to be able to concentrate," she complained to Ben.

"No doubt you will again," he said, amused.

"But Delphine can't wait."

"Well, strictly speaking, Delphine certainly can. It is you who cannot wait, since you imagine a murderer is on the loose."

"You think I'm only imagining?"

"Didn't mean it to sound that way. No, I am

with you: maybe she was murdered, maybe she wasn't. More evidence is needed."

"You know how investigations go cold. It's never good to put them aside and come back later when you feel like it."

"But this isn't a question of your not feeling like it. You're distracted—by the best thing in the whole world—which is nothing but wonderful, Molly! Keep investigating. And also—be a little gentler on yourself. And while you're doing that, tell me what in the world Manette said that's got you stewing."

"Stewing?"

Ben just raised his eyebrows and smirked.

"Here goes: Delphine got pregnant. Back in high school."

"Really?"

"Really."

"By whom?"

"Manette wouldn't tell me. Which is strange, really, since she was willing to tell me about the pregnancy. Not that she wanted to. She was quite clearly *afraid* to tell me. Just saying that little bit of information, safe and sound in her cozy farmhouse, she was looking over her shoulder as though...as though a monster was about to step out from behind a door and snatch us both away."

They sat in silence, thinking.

"Delphine didn't have the baby, I would for sure remember that," said Ben.

"She did not. The boy who got her pregnant forced her to get an abortion. And...there is definitely more to the story, but I couldn't get it out of her. Manette is quite clearly afraid—and obviously she's not afraid of Delphine being angry for talking about her business. She's afraid of some threat that is active *now*."

"Do you think this has anything to do with the strangler? I don't see a connection, just asking because villagers have to feel that he is an active threat at the moment."

"I don't know."

Another long silence.

"I am so tired of saying 'I don't know.'" Molly sighed. "I just wish—what is it with all these mystery fathers lately? Somebody has to know something..."

"You'll figure it out," said Ben, and he believed it to be so.

With those encouraging words in her ear, Molly took off for the village, her determination redoubled. Since when did she let a difficult investigation make her lose heart? She considered going to see Madame Tessier, font of all Castillac gossip, but decided to go to Lapin's first, since he was closer in age to Delphine and her friends, and might have a better idea of any relevant stories from their school days.

"What a surprise," said Lapin, but his face did not register any pleasure at seeing her.

"Is it? I can't show up anywhere these days without getting a sour welcome."

"Oh, nothing personal," said Lapin. "It's not you at all. It's just…it's the desk. I can't get over it. I will never, ever get over it."

Molly looked mystified. "The desk?"

Lapin blew a huge breath between his lips, puffing his cheeks out. "The desk I was sure was going to make me a jillionaire."

"Ah. The jillionaire desk. So what happened to it?"

"Do you pay any attention at all? As I believe I told you, it's a fake. A remarkable, stunning, gorgeous fake. Even the appraiser said it nearly fooled him, and you know they love to lord their expertise over everybody. I'm telling you, this forger was absolutely masterful. You've seen the desk. It's the same one I showed to you and your guest, the one from the States who seemed knowledgeable about antiques?"

"Ah, Rolanda."

Lapin nodded. "Well, she was fooled too."

"You don't have to worry about your reputation, Lapin. I'm sure anybody could have—"

"I just said that," snapped Lapin. "And it doesn't help that it was Albertine of all people who gave me the whole backstory to the thing. Who would ever have thought Albertine would be the Queen of Provenance?"

Molly shook her head. "I'm a little lost."

"You do know what provenance is?"

"Sort of?"

"Oh for heaven's sake, Molly, is that baby sucking your brain cells right out of your skull?"

"That seems a little strong."

"Provenance is simply a history of ownership. A chain. It allows us to know whether a piece of art or furniture is what it is claimed to be, or... not."

"Just as I thought."

They stood looking at each other. Molly was anxious to change the subject to Delphine and her friends, and Lapin wanted to continue telling the story of the desk in excruciating detail.

They narrowed their eyes at each other.

It was Molly who broke. "All right, so what did Albertine tell you?"

"Come on in the back, so you can admire it while I tell the story," he said. They made their way down a crowded aisle. "See what a beauty she is. Fake or not," said Lapin, pointing to the desk.

"It's very...fancy," said Molly. "Hey, did you

know anything about Delphine getting pregnant, back when you were in school?"

"What sort of wild goose chase are you on about now? Now listen, do you remember Albertine's aunt?"

"I didn't grow up here, remember?"

"Right, I tend to forget that," he said, with a warm smile at last. "Seems like you've always been here, harassing everyone down to their last nerve."

"Thanks?"

"Well, Albertine had an aunt. Deceased many years ago. An odd bird, a little like Albertine herself. Anyway, she got it in her head that she and Lucien Pugh were destined for romance. A mad, wild crush that as far as I know lasted until her death. She followed him around until the poor man was beside himself, he never did figure out a way to divert her attention somewhere else."

"How does the desk fit in?"

"It was commissioned by Albertine's aunt. It was intended to convince Pugh to love her, I guess, a sort of love-offering. She spent what must have been her life savings hiring a forger to make the desk, and then gave it to Lucien. A gift worth —if it had been genuine—a fortune. A dazzling piece of art! And there it sat, my beautiful little desk, in Lucien's drab living room with a stack of old magazines sitting on it, for decades. After talking to his nephew, I don't believe Lucien had any idea that the desk was supposed to be valuable. I mean, it *isn't* valuable, not like I thought—"

"—at least not jillionaire-valuable—"

"Just so." Lapin looked at the desk mournfully, then bent down and stroked his hand along the polished wood. "The forger is some kind of savant, that's what the appraiser said. Said he'd never encountered anyone so good. Lord only knows how Albertine's aunt got hold of him. And what it cost her."

"I'm sorry, Lapin."

"Me too."

"People go to such lengths to manipulate other people, don't they?"

Lapin just kept stroking the desk and did not answer.

"Why can't we just accept that other people get to make their own decisions?" said Molly.

Lapin sighed.

"So I was wondering—"

"And Lucien Pugh, of all people! Not to speak ill of the dead—but I'm going to—he was the most boring man on earth. Perfectly pleasant, I guess, not bad, never heard he was up to anything evil. Just a boring piece of plain unbuttered toast. Such an odd person to fix with such devotion. Having that desk made must have bankrupted Albertine's aunt! And for nothing!"

Molly drummed her fingers on the desk, making Lapin glare at her.

"Albertine...she was in Delphine's class, wasn't she?"

Lapin pressed his palms over his eyes. "Yes, I believe so."

"Do you think...well, let me ask this first—if you're done talking about the desk for now?"

"I will never be done talking about the desk."

"Understood," said Molly with a little smile, knowing it to be so. "What I'm wondering is—do you know of any bad blood from your school days, concerning Delphine? Just as an example: is it possible that Delphine was terribly mean to Albertine, all those years ago, and she's still holding a grudge?"

"That family seems to hold on to emotional states longer than most."

Molly nodded. Was that a tiny spark of hope erupting in her chest, at the possibility of...a possibility?

"I don't know," said Lapin. "Albertine nurses grudges about a million things. She's furious at Lucien Pugh for not marrying her aunt. She's furious at me because she wants to come into the shop, put on jewelry, and walk out without paying, which I don't, obviously, allow her to do."

He shrugged. "So could she have something to be furious with Delphine about? Honestly, I'd be surprised if she didn't."

※

ALL OF A SUDDEN, right there in Lapin's shop, Molly felt a strange sensation she had never felt before in her life.

"Oh!" she blurted, putting both hands on her stomach.

"What is it? Oh my heavens, are you having the baby right here in my shop?"

Molly laughed. "I sure hope not, I'm not nearly far enough along. I think I just felt the baby move for the first time!"

Lapin bent down next to her belly. "Hello in there!" he said, careful not to jostle her.

Molly put a hand on the top of the desk, trying to bring her attention back to Delphine and Albertine, while still savoring the little squirm and wondering if it was going to continue.

"All right. So, Albertine…" she said.

"I will say this about her—back in the day, that girl could go off. I mean, *really* lose her temper. Zero self-control. She would throw things, hit, you name it. I remember one time, she had a meltdown right in the middle of history class. She went for someone—don't remember who—the teacher had stepped out of the room and André had to wrap his arms around her to hold her back."

"Who was she attacking?"

"I don't remember. Solange Forestier could be really annoying, always thinking she's smarter than everyone else, maybe it was her. Or I guess it could have been Delphine—she was kind of the class queen, you know? I don't think she was especially mean, but Albertine might have felt...oh, I don't know what Albertine might have felt!" Lapin shook his head. "That day, André was acting like he'd saved the world from disaster. That guy—always making sure he comes out smelling like a rose, no matter what's gone down."

"You said, 'back in the day, she could go off'—are you saying Albertine doesn't do that anymore?"

"How should I know? I knew about it then because we were in school with her all day long. I have no idea what she does with herself now, I don't see her that much."

"So who did she attack that day? Come on, Lapin, think. Could it have been Delphine that Albertine went after?"

But Lapin, infuriatingly, could not say. "We're talking about thirty years ago now—no, more.

Aren't school spats from that long ago gone and forgotten by now?"

"For some people," said Molly. "But maybe... not for everybody."

After hearing a bit more about the desk, and again prodding Lapin to remember Albertine's attack in history class, Molly gave up and said her goodbyes.

Back on the street, she put on her helmet, then patted her belly, pausing, to see if she felt any more movement.

She remembered Albertine coming into Chez Papa, Albertine walking down the street, Albertine—

Wait a minute...

All of a sudden, an image flashed in Molly's mind. She straddled the scooter and headed for the Renaud farm, trying not to speed, and failing.

55

Molly jumped off before the scooter had come to a stop, nearly flinging it to the ground in her rush. But she forced herself to slow down, to breathe, and set the scooter securely on its kickstand before trotting—heart racing—to the farmhouse door.

No answer.

Molly grimaced at her mistake. They were at Lucie Severin's, of course!

She turned to leave but heard a rooster and glanced back, seeing the chicken coop on the side of the house, and then, blessedly, Gilbert emerging from the coop holding a bucket.

"Gilbert!" she called, running toward him.

"Molly, what are you running for! You shouldn't be—"

"Pregnant women can run," she laughed, touched. "Listen, is your mother here? I have to talk to her. It's important."

Gilbert's eyes got big. "What?"

"I'll tell you soon. Where's your mom?"

"She's in the barn. We just came over to feed the chickens and then we're going back to Madame Severin's." He watched Molly's face, trying to decode it.

"Okay, good. Before I talk to her—I want to say to you…Gilbert, you are a wonderful kid. Big kid. Practically a man," she added, seeing his expression. "And I want you to know that when it comes to your parents—I mean, your birth parents—and this is true for everyone—"

Gilbert looked confused.

"Sorry, I'm in a rush. What I want to say is, sure, we get some DNA from our parents, but that doesn't determine what kind of people we are. Understand me? You make your own life, Gilbert. Not your parents."

He had a million questions, but when Molly spotted Madame Renaud, she stopped him. "Stay here," she said. "I'm sorry, but for this particular thing I need to talk to your mother alone. You'll know everything very soon. If I'm right," she added.

"Cataline!" she called, waving, and walking quickly toward the woman in Castillac who disliked her the most.

56

After their talk—short and to the point—Molly wanted to hug Cataline. She could see the woman was on the verge of tears, and Molly understood that she didn't want her to see any crying.

"Just get yourselves back to Lucie's, quickly, at least for now," Molly said. "And...thank you. I know none of this has been easy."

Cataline bowed her head, then turned back towards Gilbert. Molly ran to the scooter, waved, and was about to roar off, but stopped to send Ben a quick text.

got him. headed to chantal

. . .

She knew she would make the poor man lose his mind by being so cryptic, but she couldn't help herself.

57

Right at the edge of the village, the much beloved glossy green scooter sputtered, lurched twice, stopped dead.

Out of gas.

Not now, thought Molly, trying to start it even though the gas gauge made the problem obvious. *Not now*.

She rolled the scooter out of the street and hurried towards the gendarmerie.

Her mind was swirling, seeing Chez Papa, the market, the Renaud farm, her own living room—hearing snippets of conversation she didn't understand at the time that now had new meaning.

Had the reality of what Cataline Renaud just admitted sunk in?

No.

That would take time.

But Molly was able to start doing the next right thing nonetheless. She would be relieved to hand the whole thing over to Chantal, who might need to call in some gendarmes from Bergerac—and for the moment, until the killer was apprehended, Cataline and Gilbert needed protection, and—

What was that? She turned quickly, saw no one on the deserted village street, hurried on towards the gendarmerie.

I'm letting my imagination get to me, she thought, walking even more quickly. It's unsettling when a person you've been trusting turns out to be untrustworthy. It's destabilizing. Molly whirled around again, again feeling as though someone was behind her.

Nothing.

The outer streets of the village felt isolated because there was little foot traffic. A lot of garages and small alleyways with no one around but a hungry-looking dog who lifted his head until Molly passed, then set it back down again.

Molly noticed the dog, because that was who she was, but her attention was mostly to the rear. She stopped suddenly and was almost certain she heard a single footstep, then silence. She kept going, varying her speed, a few slow steps and then a jog, then whipped around—

—maybe it *was* her imagination. The street was empty.

She took in a long, slow breath, forced her shoulders to relax. Her mind was like a rabid squirrel, jumping from one thing to the next, criticizing herself for not having seen the truth sooner, worrying about Gilbert and Cataline—

—and then just like that, his arms wrapped around her and she was dragged into the dark, his hand over her mouth. She tried to bite that hand but her teeth could not get a purchase on his flesh because he was pressing so tightly.

Ben's going to kill me, she thought, fighting against a wave of wooziness.

Do not faint, she said to herself, as sternly as she had ever in her life said anything.

Do. Not. Faint.

THEY STOOD in the dark for some long moments, his body pressed into hers from behind, his arms gripping her. Molly could feel how strong he was and did not struggle.

She waited. Thankfully, she felt the wooziness recede.

Slowly, he slid his hand from her mouth. Molly understood that he would clap it right back if she screamed.

Or worse.

She debated. Conventional wisdom said to scream, to take that risk.

But she did not. Not yet, though her heart was racing and she was as scared as she had ever been in her life.

He could kill her if he wanted to, she understood that. He could do it quickly, easily. And he had reasons to want to.

He held her arms tight to her sides, staying behind her, out of sight, but of course Molly was not confused about who he was. The question was: what did he plan to do with her? *To* her?

Her eyes were adjusting to the darkness—it was not pure dark any longer, only the dark of a garage with no windows and the door closed. She could make out shapes and they were becoming more visible moment by moment.

He did not speak. Molly guessed he was trying to decide on his next step. He could snap her neck in a second, but she pushed that thought out of her mind.

"André," said Molly, finally. Gently.

His grip tightened. She made no move to get away.

A long pause.

"Fancy meeting you here," he said into her ear, as though they had just run into each other at the opera. His tone light, even friendly.

Molly's mind was racing.

He said, almost whispering, "I wonder—I should have asked when we first met—what brought you to Castillac, Molly? How in the world did you decide on this village, of all the villages you could have moved to?" His tone, chillingly, was like honey. Like he was talking to someone he had just met at a swanky cocktail party, whom he hoped to impress. Or to someone he treasured beyond anything.

Molly forced herself to breathe slowly to slow her heart down. She tried to shrug in answer to his question, but he was holding her arms so tightly her shoulders didn't budge.

"Pure chance," she said. Her voice sounded a little more ragged than she would like. Just keep talking, she thought. Get a conversation going.

She cleared her throat. "I had an unhappy marriage. I had been looking at French real estate online, sort of a second career that turned into, to be honest." She managed a reasonably authentic chuckle. "Like I said, I was unhappy. I started fantasizing."

He squeezed her arms so hard it hurt.

"Anyway, one day I happened to see La Baraque for sale and it was love at first sight. The next thing I knew, I was here."

No response.

"If you let go of my arms, we could have a proper chat."

No response.

"And then, as I suppose you already know, I met Ben. And once we got together, there was no way I would ever leave. Castillac is part of me now, and I hope I am part of it."

"What a lovely speech," he said.

"I hope you will find the same happiness with Blanchefleur."

André made a kind of sound Molly had never heard before and hoped never to hear again. A chill went through her and she focused on her breathing to try to calm her racing heart.

She had been in some tricky spots before, but this one... She swallowed hard, trying to get control of her fear.

A car went slowly down the street, rolling right past the garage door. Molly did not make a sound. She waited.

"I am envious of you, growing up here," she said softly, and her voice surprising her by sounding confident. "I know it's not always easy. I'm sure there are...tensions, when everyone has grown up together, their lives entwined whether they wanted that or not. But you Castillacois—when the chips are down, when it matters, you support each other. Even if you don't necessarily like each other."

She tried to sense his reaction but all she had to go on was his grip, which remained strong.

"Why are you so obsessed with the past?" he said, his mouth right by her ear. "Blanchefleur doesn't need to know ancient history. Yet you go digging it all up. Ruining *everything*."

His breathing was faster. Molly imagined his heart was beating even faster than hers.

He's going to kill me, and then go straight to the Renaud farm and kill Cataline and Gilbert, thought Molly.

Stop it.

She tried to move an arm and he tightened his grip so much it felt as though her arm would snap. He had a shocking amount of strength in his hands. And she could feel his hatred, his contempt for her, radiating from his body, no matter how much honey was in his voice.

I'm screwed, a little voice said within Molly, deep down. And a little peep escaped her lips, unbidden.

58

Paul-Henri was thinking about lunch.

The Chief was in such a mood lately that he had spent the last few days on the street, not going to the gendarmerie except for first thing in the morning to see if she had any briefing for him.

But there was no briefing.

So Paul-Henri did what he usually did, which was cover all the streets of Castillac over the course of the day, chatting with villagers, keeping an eye and an ear out, hoping for an opportunity to be of service.

On that Wednesday, he happened to be walking on the outer streets of the village, deep in contemplation on the subject of lamb stew. His mother had made quite a creditable one, heavy on the sage, and he would always love it if only for the nostalgia. The ragout at the Cafe de la Place was not the same, though it too was delectable in its way—

He stopped.

The street was still.

What was that sound he just heard? Was it a cat? Cats could make the strangest noises, you'd think someone was being strangled—

—what *was* that?

He stepped close to a garage door and put his ear to it.

He heard nothing.

He took a step back. He licked his lips, wondering if he were hearing things.

Another little peep. Barely audible. But for some reason—he wanted later to explain but his action was inexplicable—he did not like the sound of that peep at all. He heard fear in it, was all he could give for explanation. He thought perhaps an animal was trapped inside the garage, and needed help.

So in a burst, Paul-Henri grabbed the garage door handle and pulled it back forcefully.

It was not a cat.

It was André Baudelaire with his arms around Molly Sutton?

What?

Quickly, while all three were in shock, Molly wrenched herself out of André's grasp. André was smiling at Paul-Henri, his palms up, starting to speak—

—and Paul-Henri, as for the rest of his life he never got tired of describing, without hesitation pulled the taser from his belt and in a flash knocked André to the ground.

He had André in handcuffs in a matter of seconds, while Molly looked on, absolutely astonished.

59

"Well, where on earth *is* Molly?" said Lapin crossly. He was at the bar at Chez Papa, having come that night even though Wednesdays were not his usual night for staying out, to find out the latest news.

"I shouldn't be surprised if she's home in bed, after a thing like that, in her condition," said Paul-Henri, his chest puffed out.

A circle of villagers pressed in on him, talking over each other, asking questions and expostulating.

"I always knew there was something off about him—"

"—with what evidence? I say we shouldn't be tasing people like that, it's downright fascist—"

"—never liked that guy—"

"Come on, Paul-Henri, tell us, what is going on! So you caught André with Molly—doing what? Were they having an affair?"

"An affair?" said Paul-Henri. "Oh sir, you misunderstand entirely. He had taken Molly hostage. If I hadn't been on patrol, as I am day in and day out—"

"*Hostage?*"

"That makes no sense at all. André is the nicest—"

The crowd was starting to get out of hand, what with so many unanswered questions and the effect of too much alcohol.

Nico slammed a tray on the bar and stunned everyone into silence.

"Listen, you lot," he said. "Chief Charlot has André in custody. Surely that would not be the case if she didn't have cause. I'm sure we'll soon find out the details—"

But the crowd was not in a listening mood. They kept pressing in on Paul-Henri—to his pleasure, on the one hand, and discomfort, on the other—and the hubbub got even louder.

Nico looked at Frances and shrugged. He turned up the music and kept slinging drinks. It was a good thing Luka had gotten over her digestive problems and could sleep through anything...it was going to be a long night.

⁂

Molly was on the sofa at La Baraque, snuggled next the Ben, the woodstove roaring against the chilly night.

"You sure you don't want to take a quick victory lap at Chez Papa?"

"I am happy right here." She leaned her head on his chest.

They lay like that for some time, looking at the fire flickering in the stove.

"You know that text you sent verged on cruel," said Ben.

Molly cackled.

"And I'm honestly having some trouble taking the whole thing in. André Baudelaire, perennial nice guy, killed Delphine and tried to kill Madame Renaud?"

"Yes. I can't exactly prove the Delphine part yet. He dragged me into that garage—what other motive could he possibly have had for that, except to shut me up? I'm sure he saw me talking to Cataline—was stalking her, because she's another woman he was desperate to shut up. Sort of perfect in a way that he tried to strangle her—literally keep her from speaking. But she was ready for him. Anyway, André was lurking and saw that we had an emotional conversation ending in a hug. André is a lot of things, but he's not stupid—I'm sure he guessed correctly that she was no longer keeping his secret."

"And once one secret is out, they all start to tumble into the light."

"Exactly. And that would be the end of Blanchefleur. Once she heard about abortions and out-of-wedlock babies, she'd take off like a rocket. With all her money, which was no doubt what André was after."

"I feel so gullible. I should have seen—"

"Oh, André's *good*. I think most of us were taken in by his charm, I was too. And also—we make the biggest mistake of all, which is assuming that other people are like us."

Ben kissed the top of her head. "You're not like anybody," he said with a laugh.

"I still need to talk to Charlot—but I suspect it was André who told her Delphine had eaten the cheese. Charlot didn't grow up in Castillac, she wouldn't have realized that Delphine would never have been socializing with André, not in a million years."

Ben shook his head and smiled. "Charlot is missing the context."

"Which in Castillac is everything." Molly sighed a deep, luxurious sigh. They lay looking at the fire, feeling safe and content. Well, and a little bit pleased with themselves.

❦

LAWRENCE WAS LOOKING STERN. "You simply cannot go around solving murder cases and then disappearing with no explanation whatsoever! I waited and waited at Chez Papa, and where were you? Lazing about thinking about nothing but that baby, that's what! What in the world will it be like once that baby is born?"

Molly laughed. She signaled to Pascal for more bread and he disappeared into the kitchen to get it.

"Quit laughing! I have questions, so many questions. So sit back and get ready to answer them, girlfriend."

Molly was ravenous and eyeing the crust of baguette on Lawrence's plate. When would the hangar steak with frites arrive?

"The funny thing is—we were saying this at Chez Papa last night, when you were absent—the consensus in the village was that André was the nicest man in the world. But...individually? When people gave their real opinion? Most people did not like him at all. Or...as you clearly found out, were frightened of him."

"Yes. And obviously for good reason."

"But how did you see through him?"

Molly looked up at the ceiling and thought about this. "I didn't, not until the last minute. I thought he and Blanchefleur were sweet together. I did know that something had happened, almost thirty years ago, something that still scared Manette and the others in her group. And so it wasn't a leap to guess that whatever it was might have had something to do with Delphine's death."

"And so? What was it?"

Molly took a deep breath and lowered her voice. "I harassed those poor women until finally Manette broke down and told me—at least part of it. Back in high school, André got Delphine pregnant."

"Uh oh."

"Well, the real uh-oh is that he not only insisted she get an abortion, but they had a big fight about it and he beat her up."

"Beat up a pregnant girl? *André?*"

"Yes. André. And when her friends went to her defense, he threatened them. Keep quiet about the pregnancy and the beating, or else. They felt that there was pretty much nothing he wouldn't do and have been terrified of him ever since. That's why

Delphine fled to New York City, to get away from him."

"And when she came back all those years later, it still wasn't safe."

"People like André—they hold grudges forever. I imagine his rage at her was as fresh in 2008 as it was in 1990. But the bigger problem for André was his fiancée. He knew if Blanchefleur heard the story of what he did to Delphine back in high school, she would vanish."

Lawrence shook his head. "What about Madame Renaud? How does she fit into this?"

"She had an affair with André twelve years ago. Well, not really affair, more like a drunken one-night stand after a village fête. And she got pregnant too. Cataline's tougher than Delphine, and she insisted on keeping the baby, but she was forced—by André—never to reveal who the father was. He has a thing about secrecy, because how else to preserve this false persona of being Mr. Good Guy?"

"Who knew Madame Renaud was such a wild thing?"

"I know, right?" said Molly, wanting to laugh but unable to get away from the sorrow of the situation. "Just horrible that she's lived all this time in such fear, always looking over her shoulder. And feeling so protective of poor Gilbert. She must have worried André might snatch him away, or hurt him, or—who knows what? And all the while, André acts like he's the kindest, most generous man alive. Half the village—the ones who had no idea what happened with Delphine, or had any other run-in with him—bought that act too. He was smooth as silk, I'll give him that."

Pascal arrived with two baguettes and put them on the table before scurrying off to seat some customers. Molly tore in to the baguette with delight, not sparing the butter.

"But Molly, you haven't explained what put you onto André. Where was the crack that allowed you to see him for what he is?"

She smiled as well as she could with her mouth full. "The tiniest little thing. He was at La Baraque for dinner, just him and Blanchefleur, me and Ben. And I yawned—a mighty, pregnant lady yawn. As I did so, Ben started to yawn. Blanchefleur yawned. Yawning is notably contagious, you know."

"Yes, I do know. Just your talking about it is making me do it," he said, yawning.

"Exactly. It's curious, isn't it? But the thing is—and I noticed it at the time, though didn't really know that I noticed, if you understand what I mean—André sat at a table with three other people yawning like mad, and he...just sat there. Blank face. No yawn."

Lawrence looked mystified.

"And I read somewhere that it's a tell for sociopaths. They don't have any connection to other people, and so are impervious to yawning when other people do."

"Just a little light reading, Molly?"

"I'm having a baby, not a brain transplant." She laughed, and clapped her hands at the sight of Pascal headed their way with plates piled high with steak and frites.

EPILOGUE

The aftereffects of the arrest of André Baudelaire took some time to die down.

Gilbert Renaud, not surprisingly, struggled with the news of who his father was, and took his anger out on his mother, who accepted the anger with fortitude and even gratitude, because she was so relieved André was in prison and she no longer had to worry so much about Gilbert's safety.

Delphine's body was exhumed and various tests performed, which showed that her heart attack had been caused by the ingestion of aluminum phosphide, a common and readily available rat poison. Paul-Henri, continuing his professional winning streak, managed to find the shop—all the way in Bordeaux—where André had purchased it. Of course there was no one to testify to seeing André force Delphine to eat the tablets, but the court was persuaded that that was what he had done.

Blanchefleur was by turns ecstatic that she had dodged a bullet and horrified that she had very nearly turned over control of her finances to the "murdering bastard," as she called him, refusing to use his name ever again.

Chief Charlot considered investigating the death of André's first wife, Marianne, who had died by falling over a cliff during a hiking trip in the Cevennes. It had been just the two of them hiking alone. Eventually Charlot decided there was no way to gather any evidence since the only eyewitness was the suspect himself. But the village did not hesitate to convict him, outside of the courts.

And last, Florian Nagrand was thrilled about Selma's return and the prospect of his first child. And also morose, because Selma was not altogether sure she wanted to settle in Castillac for good.

"It does seem rather a dangerous place," she was overheard saying at Chez Papa, and really, no one could argue the point.

GLOSSARY

CHAPTER 1

tais-toi......................shut up

Chapter 2
    pigeonnier...................pigeon house, renovated as a living space
    hola..........................hello
    goutez.......................taste
    tempête......................tempest

Chapter 3
    va-t'en......................go away
    chérie.......................dear, dearest

GLOSSARY

Chapter 4
notaire..................French official, handles real estate transactions and other matters
maman......................mother

Chapter 7
verklempt....................overcome with emotion (Yiddish)

Chapter 8
merde........................poop (mildly vulgar)

Chapter 10
le déluge......................the flood

Chapter 12
dévoté........................fan
épicerie......................small grocery
n'est-ce pas....................right? (Is it not?)

Chapter 14
daube........................Provençal beef stew

Chapter 15
au contraire....................to the contrary

Chapter 17
énchanté......................enchanted

GLOSSARY

gratin dauphinoise..............sliced potatoes baked in cream

Chapter 18
    auf wiedersen....................goodbye (German)

Chapter 19
    brocante........................flea market
    primaire........................grade school

Chapter 23
    manoir........................manor

Chapter 32
    cantine........................school cafeteria
    Père Noël......................Santa Claus
    le prof...........................teacher
    bûche de noël...................Christmas log, a special holiday cake make to look like a log

Chapter 34
    apéro................................cocktail party

Chapter 35
    ça va............................how are you?

Chapter 38
    mairie..........................town hall

GLOSSARY

Chapter 42
    boulevardier......................man about town
    la Belle Epoque...................."The beautiful age" just before World War I

Chapter 45
    mec...............................guy, fellow

ACKNOWLEDGMENTS

Big thanks to Tommy Glass, Nancy Kelley, Paul Ardoin, Nellie Baumer, and Lisa Carlisle. Couldn't do it without you.

ABOUT THE AUTHOR

Nell Goddin has worked as a radio reporter, SAT tutor, short-order omelet chef, and baker. She tried waitressing but was fired twice.

Nell grew up in Richmond, Virginia and has lived in New England, New York City, and France. She has degrees from Dartmouth College and Columbia University.

www.goddinbooks.com
nell@goddinbooks.com

ALSO BY NELL GODDIN

The Third Girl (Molly Sutton Mysteries 1)
The Luckiest Woman Ever (Molly Sutton Mysteries 2)
The Prisoner of Castillac (Molly Sutton Mysteries 3)
Murder for Love (Molly Sutton Mysteries 4)
The Château Murder (Molly Sutton Mysteries 5)
Murder on Vacation (Molly Sutton Mysteries 6)
An Official Killing (Molly Sutton Mysteries 7)
Death in Darkness (Molly Sutton Mysteries 8)
No Honor Among Thieves (Molly Sutton Mysteries 9)
Eye for an Eye (Molly Sutton Mysteries 10)
Bittersweet Oblivion (Molly Sutton Mysteries 11)
Seven Corpses All in a Row (Molly Sutton Mysteries 12)

You can get Nell's books at goddinbooks.com, at all major online retailers, or ask for them at your local bookstore.

Sign up for news and discounts at goddinbooks.com

Printed in the USA
CPSIA information can be obtained
at www.ICGtesting.com
LVHW091137020824
787115LV00038B/552